I0822160

THE ICE CREATURE

The Ice Creature

ISBN: 979-8-9907254-2-3 (hardback)
979-8-9907254-3-0 (paperback)

Printed in the United States of America

THE ICE CREATURE

GARY J. ROSE

DEDICATION

To my sister, for being the first to read this manuscript and catching the errors I had missed. Your keen eye and unwavering support have been invaluable.

And to my recently departed dog, Churnish, who, like Old Yeller, was the "best doggone dog in the world." You laid at my feet as I completed this novel, offering companionship and comfort every step of the way. You are forever missed.

"The cold has a way of seeping
into your bones, but it's the unknown
that chills the soul."

—The Author

HOMAGE

As a young boy of seven years old, I watched the movie *The Thing from Another World*. At that time, it terrified me beyond belief. It was produced during what I consider the golden age of horror and science-fiction films. Most were filmed in black and white, yet they still sent shivers down my spine as I watched.

Movies such as *King Kong*, *Godzilla*, *The Day the Earth Stood Still*, *The Fly*, *Invasion of the Body Snatchers*, *War of the Worlds*, *Them!*, *House on Haunted Hill*, *The Tingler*, *Frankenstein*, *Dracula*, *The Wolfman*, and *Twenty Million Miles to Earth*, to name a few, are considered classics today by horror and Science Fiction enthusiasts.

The Thing from Another World, sometimes referred to simply as *The Thing*, is a 1951 American black-and-white science fiction-horror film directed by Christian Nyby, produced by Edward Lasker for Howard Hawks' Winchester Pictures Corporation, and released by RKO Radio Pictures.

The film stars Margaret Sheridan, Kenneth Tobey, Robert Cornthwaite, and Douglas Spencer. James

Arness plays the titular role of The Thing. *The Thing from Another World* is based on the 1938 novella "Who Goes There?" by John W. Campbell (writing under the pseudonym of Don A. Stuart).

The film's storyline follows a United States Air Force crew and scientists who discover a crashed flying saucer frozen in the Arctic ice, along with a humanoid body nearby. Returning to their remote Arctic research outpost with the body still encased in a block of ice, they must defend themselves against the malevolent, plant-based alien when it is accidentally thawed out.

In Anchorage, journalist Ned Scott, seeking a story, visits the officer's club of the Alaskan Air Command. There, he meets Captain Pat Hendry, his co-pilot, and flight navigator. General Fogarty orders Hendry to fly to Polar Expedition Six at the North Pole in response to a request from its lead scientist, Nobel laureate Dr. Arthur Carrington, who has reported that an unusual aircraft has crashed nearby. With Scott, Corporal Barnes, crew chief Bob, and a pack of sled dogs, Hendry pilots a Douglas C-47 Skytrain transport aircraft to the remote outpost.

Upon arrival, Scott and the airmen meet radio operator Tex, scientists Dr. Chapman and his wife, and colleagues Vorhees, Stern, Redding, Stone, Laurence, Wilson, Ambrose, and Carrington. Hendry later rekindles his romance with Nikki Nicholson, Carrington's secretary.

Several scientists fly with the airmen to the crash site, where they find a large object buried beneath the ice. As they spread out to determine the object's shape, they realize they are standing in a circle, outlining a flying saucer. The team attempts to free it from the ice with thermite, but a violent reaction with the craft's metal alloy completely destroys it. However, their Geiger counter detects something buried nearby—a frozen body. It is excavated intact in a large block of ice and flown back to the base as an Arctic storm closes in.

Given the discovery, Hendry assumes command of the outpost. Pending radio instructions from General Fogarty, he denies Scott permission to send out his story and the scientists' demands to examine the body. Tex sends an update to Fogarty, and the airmen settle in for the storm.

A watch is posted; Barnes, on relieving the first shift, is disturbed by the creature's glare through the clearing ice and covers it with an electric blanket he does not realize is plugged in. The block slowly thaws, and the creature, still alive, escapes into the storm. It fights with the sled dogs, killing two but losing most of its right forearm.

An airman recovers the stump after the attack, and the scientists examine its tissue, concluding that the creature is an advanced form of plant life. Carrington is convinced of its superiority to humans and becomes intent on communicating with it. The airmen begin a search, which leads to the outpost's greenhouse. Carrington stays behind with other scientists, having noticed evidence of alien activity there. They discover a hidden third sled dog, which had been bled dry, revealing the creature as a vampire that feeds on blood. Carrington and the scientists post a secret watch of their own, hoping to encounter it before the airmen do.

The next morning, the airmen continue their search. Tex informs them that Fogarty is aware of their discovery and demands further information, now prevented by the fierce storm. Stern appears, badly injured, and tells the group that the creature has killed and bled two scientists. When the airmen investigate, they are attacked but manage to barricade the creature inside the greenhouse. Hendry confronts Carrington and orders him to remain in his lab and quarters.

Obsessed with the creature, Carrington shows Nicholson and the other scientists that he has been growing small alien plants from seeds taken from the severed arm and feeding them with the base's blood plasma supply. Hendry discovers the theft when plasma is needed to treat Stern, which leads him to Carrington.

Fogarty transmits orders to keep the creature alive, but it escapes from the greenhouse and attacks the airmen in their quarters. They douse it with buckets of kerosene and set it aflame, forcing it to retreat into the -60°F storm. After regrouping, they realize the creature has sabotaged the base furnaces' oil supply, plummeting temperatures indoors. They retreat to the station's generator room to keep warm and rig a high-voltage electrical "fly trap."

The creature continues to stalk them. At the last moment, Carrington pleads with it but is knocked violently aside. The creature walks into the trap and is electrocuted. On Hendry's order, it is reduced to a pile of ash.

When the weather clears, Hendry and Nicholson are careening toward marriage, and Scotty is finally able to radio his "story of a lifetime" to a roomful of reporters in Anchorage. He ends his broadcast with the warning: "Tell the world. Tell this to everybody, wherever they are. Watch the skies everywhere. Keep looking. Keep watching the skies..."

Since the 1951 production, there have been two remakes of this film, both titled *The Thing*, released in 1982 and 2011. These versions are set in Antarctica, aligning with the original "Who Goes There?" story. Interestingly, the 2011 film serves as a prequel to the 1982 version. Both remakes offer a distinct take on the original film.

Inspired by these timeless classics and the enduring allure of the unknown, I set out to create a contemporary reimagining of *The Thing from Outer Space*. My novel, *The Ice Creature*, transports the terror from the icy wastelands of Antarctica to the frigid expanses of the Arctic.

Here, a team of scientists uncovers an ancient alien relic buried deep in the ice. This relic, however, is not merely an artifact; it awakens a deadly ice creature that has lain dormant for a millennia.

CHAPTER 1

In the vast, icy expanse of the Arctic wilderness, snow and ice stretch as far as the eye can see, an endless sea of white under a sky that seems perpetually overcast. The biting wind howls across the desolate landscape, carrying with it the promise of untold secrets buried deep beneath the ice.

In the distance, a lone snowmobile carves a path through the pristine snow, a solitary figure navigating the frozen terrain with practiced ease. The hum of the engine is almost lost in the roar of the wind, but it perseveres, a beacon of human determination in an unforgiving environment. The driver, bundled in layers of thick, insulated gear, leans into the machine, urging it forward toward the destination.

Ahead, the remote research facility looms, a cluster of prefabricated buildings huddled together as if for warmth against the encroaching cold. The structures, with their utilitarian design, seem almost dwarfed by the vast, frozen expanse surrounding them. A United States flag flaps vigorously in the strengthening wind, its stars and stripes a stark contrast against the monochrome surroundings. Beside it, an air sock spins wildly, its direction changing with the howling gusts, mirroring the unpredictable nature of the Arctic winds.

The facility, a bastion of scientific inquiry, stands as humanity's outpost at the edge of the world, where the known meets the unknown. The buildings, interconnected by covered walkways, form a small, self-contained community, with lights flickering in the windows, hinting at the activity within. The hum of generators provides a constant, reassuring presence, a reminder of the fragile lifeline that keeps the cold at bay.

The wind, ever-present and relentless, carries with it a sense of foreboding, as if whispering secrets of the ancient ice. It howls through the narrow gaps between buildings, creating an eerie symphony that echoes across the desolate landscape. The facility, though equipped with the latest technology and resources, feels like a solitary beacon of civilization in an otherwise untamed wilderness, where nature's harsh elements constantly test the resolve of those who dare to venture into its domain.

Inside the main building, Captain Tom Mitchell peers through the frosted window, watching the approaching snowmobile with a mixture of anticipation and unease. The Arctic, with its deceptive beauty, had always been a place of both fascination and fear for him. It was a realm where nature's wrath was ever-present, and the line between survival and disaster was razor-thin.

Mitchell turns away from the window and checks his watch. The rider should be Dr. Alice Warren, returning from a reconnaissance mission to investigate an unusual signal picked up by their instruments. The signal had piqued the interest of the entire team, promising a potential discovery that could put their names in the annals of scientific history. But in the Arctic, excitement was always tempered by caution.

As the snowmobile pulls up to the facility, the rider dismounts and removes their helmet, revealing Dr. Warren's determined face, flushed from the cold. She shakes her long black hair and quickly secures the snowmobile, heading towards the entrance, bracing herself against the gusting wind. The rest of the team, alerted by the sound of the engine, gathers in the common area, their curiosity palpable.

Three figures, bundled in heavy cold-weather gear, exited the building and stepped into the harsh, frigid environment of the Arctic. The wind whipped around them, carrying icy particles that stung their exposed skin and bit through the layers of insulation. Their faces, shielded by thick, fur-lined hoods, peeked out from behind goggles that protected their eyes from the blinding glare of the snow and ice.

They moved with the practiced efficiency of those well-acquainted with the merciless conditions, their steps measured and deliberate to conserve energy and maintain balance on the treacherous, uneven ground. Each carried a sturdy, insulated pack filled with essential gear, from survival tools to scientific instruments, ready for any challenge the unforgiving landscape might present.

The sound of their breathing, amplified by the cold air, mingled with the howling wind, creating a symphony of human struggle against nature's relentless assault. Frost clung to their exhalations, forming small clouds that quickly dissipated into the biting air. The wind, ever-present and capricious, seemed to toy with them, swirling around their legs and tugging at their clothing, as if trying to pull them into the icy abyss.

As they trudged forward, their boots crunching through the crust of snow, they navigated around snowdrifts and patches of exposed ice. Their hands, gloved and ready, occasionally brushed against their gear to ensure everything remained secure. Despite the oppressive cold, a sense of determination and purpose propelled them onward. Each step, a testament to their resilience and fortitude, brought them closer to their goal in the vast, desolate expanse of the Arctic wilderness.

Leading the group was Captain Mitchell, early forties, short cut blond hair, built like an NFL linebacker. Behind him was Dr. Marcus Lee, a rugged man in his fifties with a bear-like presence and a thick mustache that bristled with frost. His broad shoulders and determined stride gave him an air of authority that was hard to ignore. Behind him walked Dr. Frank Silva, a seasoned medical doctor in his sixties. His face, lined with years of experience, held a calm determination as he trudged through the snow.

As they approached the snowmobile, Dr. Warren, a striking woman in her thirties with sharp features and eyes that gleamed with intelligence and curiosity, wrapped her arms around herself. The biting cold penetrated even her heavy-duty parka, but she scarcely noticed, her mind preoccupied with the task ahead.

The lead xenobiologist of the team, Alice exuded a confidence born of both expertise and passion for her work. Her dark hair, pulled back into a practical bun, peeked out from under her fur-lined hood, and her cheeks were flushed from the cold.

Her breath formed little clouds as she exhaled, her thoughts racing with anticipation. Alice had spent years preparing for this mission, and every moment brought her closer to uncovering the secrets buried deep within the ice. Despite the harsh conditions, her determination never wavered, a testament to her resilience and commitment to her field.

"Dr. Warren," Lee greeted, his voice carrying over the howl of the wind. "Did you find anything?"

Alice nodded, her breath forming clouds in the freezing air. "Yes, Dr. Lee. It's incredible. We need to bring the others up to speed immediately."

The fourth figure, standing a bit apart from the rest, was Elena Martinez. A striking Latina, she was the youngest team member. She watched the exchange with keen interest, her own excitement barely contained. As the newest member of the team, she had quickly adapted to the rigors of their mission, driven by the same relentless curiosity that bound them all together. A communications expert as well as a gifted technology wizard, she was the life blood between the research center and civilization.

Together, they headed back towards the main building, their minds racing with the possibilities of what Alice had discovered. The Arctic landscape, vast and unyielding, seemed to close in around them, heightening the sense of urgency that propelled them forward.

Dr. Lee squinted against the biting wind, his thick mustache twitching with impatience. "Where is the rest of the team?" he asked, his voice gruff.

"They'll be here shortly," Alice replied, her breath visible in the frigid air. "They're towing several objects, so they had to go slow."

Captain Mitchell stepped forward and raised his binoculars to scan the horizon. "You should have stayed together," he admonished. "There's a storm coming in at any moment."

Dr. Lee nodded, but his mind was elsewhere. "How far down did you have to go to retrieve the relic?" he asked Alice, his eyes glinting with excitement. "This could be the find of the century."

Before Alice could respond, Captain Mitchell lowered his binoculars and pointed towards the distance. "Here they come," he announced.

Captain Mitchell pointed to the west. Everyone shaded their eyes and looked in that direction. Five additional snowmobiles approached the research facility, some towing trailers laden with securely strapped objects.

Dr. Lee, his curiosity piqued, turned to Alice. "What else did you find?"

Alice's eyes sparkled with a mix of excitement and disbelief. "You won't believe it. When we tracked down the frequency emanating from the relic, we found objects scattered over a large area. They obviously came from an alien spacecraft. We also found footprints."

"An alien spacecraft," Dr. Lee repeated, his voice filled with awe. "Outstanding!" The team stirred with a mix of excitement and apprehension, their minds racing with the implications of Alice's discovery.

Alice's voice trembled slightly as she spoke, not from fear but from the cold. "We gathered up what we could, including the relic. We took photos of the footprints, but the weather was turning for the worse."

"Footprints?" Captain Mitchell's brow furrowed in confusion.

Alice nodded. “Yes. Can I get out of the cold and get some coffee in me? Then I’ll tell you everything.” The approaching snowmobiles drew closer, carrying the precious cargo of alien artifacts. Everyone gathered around the snowmobiles, eager to get a good look at the extraordinary finds.

Dr. Silva, ever the cautious one, turned to the captain. “Captain, can I suggest that the objects be placed in quarantine? We don’t know what we are dealing with.”

“Good idea, Doctor,” Captain Mitchell agreed. He raised his voice to address the team. “Listen up, everyone. We don’t know the origin of these items. They must be placed in quarantine immediately.”

He pointed to a secure area near the facility, ensuring that everyone understood the importance of the directive. The team, buzzing with a mixture of excitement and apprehension, moved quickly to follow his orders.

“Take everything over there and make sure it’s secure in the containment building,” Captain Mitchell ordered, pointing towards the designated area. The crew nodded and began to unload the alien artifacts, moving them carefully to the quarantine area. As they worked, Elena Garcia, a tech expert in her twenties, burst out of the compound and rushed up to Captain Mitchell, her face flushed with urgency.

“Captain, all of our comms just went down. We can’t transmit or receive,” she reported breathlessly.

"Did you recalibrate everything? The storm hasn't arrived yet, so that can't be the cause. Run a diagnostic again," Mitchell instructed.

"I did, three times. It's not our equipment. I can't explain why nothing is working," Elena replied, her frustration evident.

"Alright. Everyone inside. Elena, I'll be right with you," Captain Mitchell said, his tone decisive.

He turned to Alice, his expression serious. "Listen up. No one is to move any of the items Dr. Warren brought back from the containment area without my explicit permission. Understood?"

The team members exchanged uneasy glances but nodded in agreement. They began to file into the research facility, the tension palpable in the cold, Arctic air.

CHAPTER 2

As they entered the research facility's command center, the team members made a beeline to the facility's dining area for the coffee and refreshments, eager to shake off the chill of the Arctic air. Captain Mitchell's voice cut through the hum of conversation. "In five minutes, I want everyone in the briefing room. No exceptions."

Elena leaned in close to Alice, her voice a conspiratorial whisper. "Tom can be a real asshole sometimes." Alice suppressed a smile and nodded, understanding the frustration but knowing the importance of their work.

"Yeah, he means well, but his bedside manner could use some work," Alice replied, sharing a quiet laugh with Elena. Inside the large briefing room, the entire research team had gathered, their attention focused on Captain Mitchell as he stood at the front.

"Alright, everyone, settle down," Captain Mitchell began, his voice carrying authority and calm. The room fell silent as the team focused their attention on him. "Dr. Warren, please explain what you and your team discovered."

Dr. Warren stepped forward, cradling her coffee, the warmth seeping through the mug offering a small comfort against the chill that seemed to pervade even the heated room. She took a deep breath before she began, gathering her thoughts. "Thank you, Captain," she said, her voice steady and clear.

"As you know, Elena and I have been monitoring a unique frequency for some time. This frequency was emanating from what we're labeling the relic." She paused, letting the weight of her words settle over the group. The term "relic" carried with it an air of mystery and significance, hinting at the ancient and possibly extraterrestrial origins of the object they had uncovered.

Dr. Warren's eyes scanned the room, meeting the gaze of each team member. Their faces reflected a mix of curiosity and concern, mirroring her own feelings. "The frequency itself is unlike anything we've encountered before," she continued. "It's not just a signal; it's a pattern, a sequence that suggests some form of intelligence or purpose behind it."

She took another sip of her coffee, the steam rising in delicate tendrils, and set the mug down on a nearby table. "Our initial analysis indicates that the relic could be a communication device, possibly even a beacon. The implications of this are staggering. If we're right, it means we're not just dealing with a piece of ancient technology but potentially with a message from another civilization."

The room buzzed with murmurs of excitement and disbelief. Captain Mitchell raised his hand for silence. "What does this mean for our mission?" he asked, his expression serious.

Dr. Warren nodded, appreciating the gravity of the question. "It means we need to proceed with extreme caution," she replied. "We don't fully understand the relic's capabilities or its origins. Our next step is to isolate the relic in a controlled environment and conduct further tests to decipher the frequency and its purpose."

She looked around the room, seeing the determination mirrored in the eyes of her colleagues. "This discovery could redefine our understanding of history and our place in the universe," she said, her voice filled with a mix of awe and responsibility. "But we must remain vigilant. The relic has already shown signs of influencing our environment, and we cannot predict what further exposure might entail."

Captain Mitchell nodded, his expression resolute. "Thank you, Dr. Warren. We'll take every precaution. Our mission remains to explore and understand, but above all, to ensure the safety of our team. Let's proceed with careful consideration and respect for the unknown forces we're dealing with."

As Dr. Warren stepped back before continuing, the team members exchanged glances, their minds racing with the possibilities and challenges ahead. The room, once a place of routine briefings, now felt like the center of a pivotal moment in human history.

She paused, ensuring everyone was following her explanation. "Using the radio waves from the relic, we traced it to a location further east. When we arrived, we found what appeared to be a crash site. The scene was chaotic—debris scattered over a vast area." The room fell silent, everyone hanging on her words, and the seriousness discovery sinking in.

"Most of the spacecraft was obliterated," Alice continued, her voice steady despite the weight of her words. "But we recovered several intact objects along with the relic itself. The extent of the damage indicates a violent impact. We also discovered footprints leading away from the crash site, but we lost their trail in the falling snow." She glanced at Captain Mitchell, who gave a nod for her to continue.

"Given the nature of the objects and the relic's signal, we are confident these are remnants of an alien spacecraft," Alice said, her tone serious. "This discovery is monumental, but it also demands that we proceed with extreme caution."

Dr. Lee leaned forward, his interest piqued. "I'd like to hear more about these footprints you found."

Alice looked at Captain Mitchell, who gave a nod of approval.

"If you want to gather around, here are the photos we took," she said, spreading the images on the table. "I'll have Elena enlarge them later. The footprints measure over 13 inches, and the stride between steps is an astonishing 5 feet."

Dr. Silva, unable to contain his amazement, spoke up. "That is extraordinary. In all my studies, I have never heard of a humanoid coming close to those dimensions."

The team members, except for Captain Mitchell, gathered around the table, examining the photos. Small talk broke out among them, a mix of excitement and speculation about what these discoveries could mean.

"Thank you, Dr. Warren," Captain Mitchell said, his tone firm. "This is a major discovery, but our priority is safety. As I said, no one is to touch any of these items without my direct approval."

He paused, allowing the seriousness of his words to settle over the room. "Alright, let's get to work. We have a lot to do, and we need to move quickly. Dr. Warren, please lead us to the containment building so we can examine your findings. I want security doubled at all access and egress points."

The team murmured in agreement, the weight of the situation clear on their faces. They understood the importance of what lay ahead and the necessity of proceeding with caution.

"I forgot to inform you that, for some unexplained reason, all communications are down," Captain

Mitchell announced, his voice tense. "Elena conducted a thorough diagnostic on our systems, but nothing is working. No internet, no radios, nothing. Normally, I would have immediately called for a media blackout to keep this discovery under wraps. But not only can't I do that, I also can't contact headquarters to report our findings." He paused and established eye contact with everyone.

As the team dispersed and started to head towards the containment building, Dr. Marcus Lee leaned in towards Alice, his frustration evident.

"Who the hell does Captain Mitchell think he is, telling us scientists when and where we can examine the relic and spacecraft debris?" he grumbled. "If comms weren't down, I'd contact headquarters and file a complaint. What an asshole."

Alice looked a bit surprised by Dr. Lee's outburst but quickly tried to smooth things over. "Marcus, I understand your frustration. But Captain Mitchell is just trying to ensure our safety and manage the situation. Given the circumstances, I think it's best we work together and follow protocols. Let's focus on the discoveries we've made and the potential they hold."

Dr. Lee took a deep breath, nodding reluctantly. "Yeah, you're right, Alice. Let's get to it."

The tension eased slightly as they continued towards the containment building, their focus shifting back to the remarkable discoveries awaiting them.

The team entered the containment building, their footsteps echoing in the cold, sterile environment. They walked around various tables displaying the remains of the alien craft, each piece more enigmatic than the last.

In the center of the room, a block of thick ice sat on a reinforced table. Within the ice, barely visible, was a round object that Dr. Warren had labeled "RELIC". The ice around it seemed to shimmer slightly, hinting at the mysterious power contained within. Everyone gathered around, eyes fixed on the relic, the air thick with anticipation and unease.

"So, this is the relic?" Captain Mitchell remarked, squinting at the object. "Looks like a hubcap to me." He chuckled. "What do you think these strange markings mean?"

"We're not sure yet," Alice replied. "Elena and I have tried to penetrate the ice for a better view, but we decided it's safer to let it thaw naturally to avoid any damage. By tomorrow, the ice should have melted significantly, and we'll be able to see the markings more clearly."

Captain Mitchell turned to Elena. "Elena, does any of our working equipment tell us more about the storm's approach?"

"All I can tell you is that the temperature has dropped significantly in the past hour, and the winds have really picked up," Elena reported, her voice strained. “I’d say within the next hour, we’ll be hit with the main force.” She started to cough.

Captain Mitchell glanced at Elena and then at his watch. “Dr. Silva, please check on Elena. That sounds like a nasty cough to me. Let’s adjourn to the dining room and get a hot meal. Tomorrow, we can dive deeper into the mystery of the items in the containment building. For now, I need a hot shower,” Captain Mitchell said, heading towards the exit.

He left the containment building, but a few team members remained behind for one last look at the enigmatic objects before heading out, leaving Dr. Alice Warren alone with her thoughts and the relic.

Alice lingered, her eyes fixed on the relic encased in ice. The room was quiet, the air thick with anticipation and unease. Suddenly, she heard a faint whisper.

“Alice...”

She turned, her heart pounding. Standing before her was the ghostly figure of her deceased father, his eyes filled with urgency.

“Dad? How... how is this possible?” she stammered.

“Alice, you need to leave this place. It’s not safe,” her father warned.

Alice blinked, trying to comprehend what she was seeing. As she watched, the apparition of her father began to decay, his flesh rotting away to reveal bones and decay until he vanished completely.

She gasped, stumbling back, her breath coming in rapid, shallow bursts. “What just happened?” she whispered, trying to shake off the haunting image. "I need to get some rest," she murmured to herself. With a final glance at the relic, she left the containment building, the unsettling experience weighing heavily on her mind.

CHAPTER 3

Captain Mitchell stood under the hot cascade of the shower, letting the water wash away the tension of the day. He was unaware that Alice had quietly entered his quarters. Silently, she undressed and slid open the shower curtain, surprising him.

He turned, a smile spreading across his face. "Well, this is a surprise."

"Thought you might need some company. After all, it's been a long day," Alice replied, stepping into the shower. The steam enveloped them both, creating a cocoon of warmth and intimacy.

They stood close, the water mixing with their whispered words. "You know, this alien find... it's incredible. But it worries me too," Tom admitted, his brow furrowed.

"I know. It's like nothing we've ever seen. But right now, I don't want to think about that," Alice said, her hand tracing the outline of his jaw. Tom's eyes softened, and he pulled her closer.

"Maybe you're right. We deserve a break," he murmured.

Their lips met, the kiss deepening as the water poured over them. They explored each other, the day's tension melting away in their embrace. The chemistry between them ignited, leading to an intimate moment shared in the warmth of the shower.

As they pulled back slightly, Tom looked into her eyes, his expression serious yet tender. "We'll figure it out, Alice. Together."

"Yes, together," she agreed, feeling a sense of resolve and comfort in his words. They continued their intimate connection, the outside world and its mysteries momentarily forgotten as they lost themselves in each other.

Alice and Elena, both dressed in white lab coats, stood over the now completely thawed relic. Various scientific instruments were attached to the mysterious object, their monitors flickering erratically.

"I'm picking up unusual energy readings. This thing is active," Elena said, her voice tinged with awe and concern.

Alice leaned in closer, her breath visible in the frigid air of the containment building. The relic emitted a deep, resonating pulse, and the lights flickered ominously. Suddenly, Alice's vision blurred, and she stumbled, a cold sweat breaking out on her forehead.

Her surroundings shifted. The air grew colder, and a sinister presence filled the room. She saw her late husband, Danny, standing at the lab's entrance, his face twisted into a grotesque smile.

"Alice, you need to leave this place. Now," Danny's voice echoed, distorted and unnatural. His flesh began to decay before her eyes, maggots crawling out of his rotting skin. The sight was horrifying, and Alice felt a scream rising in her throat.

Suddenly, she was jolted back to reality by Elena shaking her arm, her face etched with fear. "Dr. Warren! Alice! Are you okay?"

Alice gasped, her heart pounding. She steadied herself, her eyes darting to the relic as it pulsed again, casting eerie, shifting shadows that seemed to move of their own accord. "I... I saw Danny. My husband. He was here. He told me to leave. You didn't see him?"

Elena's eyes widened, the color draining from her face. The relic's pulsing grew more intense, and the instruments around them started to glitch, emitting a high-pitched whine.

"No, I didn't see anything. We need to get out of here. Now," Elena said, her voice trembling. The room grew darker, the shadows deepening as a sense of impending doom enveloped them. The relic pulsed once more, sending a shockwave through the building and causing the lights to flicker violently.

They scrambled towards the exit, the containment building now filled with an overwhelming, malevolent energy that threatened to consume everything within its walls. The door would not open.

"What is going on?" Elena asked, her voice filled with fear as she and Alice pounded on the door.

Alice shook her head, her expression grim. "It's worse than we thought, Elena. The frequency... it's not just a signal. It's a call."

"A call? To what?" Elena asked, her voice tense.

Alice sighed deeply. "To something out there. Something that might be coming here."

Elena's eyes widened in fear. She glanced at the relic, then back at Alice. "We need to tell Captain Mitchell. Now."

Captain Mitchell sat in the control room, his eyes fixed on the security feeds. The monitors displayed various angles of the containment building, but it was the sight of Elena and Alice pounding on the exit door that caught his attention. Frowning, he turned on the audio feed to the room.

"What's going on there?" his voice crackled through the speakers.

"We need to get out of here. Captain, we have a serious problem. The relic... it's not just emitting a frequency. It's sending a call," Elena shouted, her voice filled with urgency.

"A call? To what?" Captain Mitchell's voice came through the intercom, tense and concerned.

"We don't know yet," Alice spoke quickly, her words tumbling over each other. "But it's possible that whatever it's calling could be dangerous. We can't take any risks."

Captain Mitchell paused, considering the gravity of the situation. He turned to his communication officer. "Attention all personnel. We are initiating a full lockdown of the containment building. No one in or out until further notice. Security team to the containment building. Dr. Warren and Elena are trapped inside."

"Yes, sir. Lockdown initiated," the communication officer responded, acknowledging the order.

Alarms blared as the containment building door was forced open. Captain Mitchell quickly approached Elena and Alice, his expression serious.

"Are you two, okay?" he asked, concern evident in his voice.

Elena and Alice nodded, their faces reflecting the weight of the situation. "The relic somehow trapped us inside," Alice said, still shaken by the experience.

"Calm down. It's just a hunk of metal. How could it force the door shut?" Captain Mitchell questioned, skepticism in his voice.

"Tom, this thing is evil. I don't understand how, but it manipulated the door shut. And I've just experienced my second hallucination," Alice said, her voice trembling with frustration and fear.

"Hallucinations? Why haven't you told me about this before?" Captain Mitchell demanded, his concern deepening.

"Because every time we bring up our concerns, you dismiss them," Alice retorted, her frustration boiling over. "This isn't just about strange readings or unexplained phenomena. This relic is affecting us, and we need to take it seriously before someone gets hurt."

Elena nodded in agreement, her face serious. "She's right, Captain. We need to figure out what we're dealing with, and we need your support to do it."

Captain Mitchell looked between them, seeing the genuine fear and frustration in their eyes. He took a deep breath, his expression softening slightly. "Alright. First, Alice, you are off to sick bay. I want Dr. Silva to check you out. Next, we'll take every precaution necessary. Let's figure this out together."

Alice and Elena exchanged relieved glances, the weight of the situation still heavy but now shared.

CHAPTER 4

In the containment building, the room was dimly lit, the air thick with tension. Captain Mitchell stood at the head of a long table, looking haggard and uncertain. Around him sat Alice, Dr. Lee, and several other team members. The relic, securely locked in a containment chamber nearby, emitted a faint, eerie glow that seeped into the room.

Captain Mitchell raised his voice, trying to command the room's attention. "Alright, everyone, listen up. We're in uncharted territory here. That... thing is locked down, but it's clear we don't fully understand what we're dealing with. I need everyone to report on what they've experienced so far."

Alice, pale but composed, spoke up. "I've had hallucinations. My deceased father and husband appeared to me, warning us to leave. I've also noticed a significant drop in temperature around the relic."

Captain Mitchell looked at Dr. Silva, hoping for his input.

"Alice is fine," Dr. Silva said. "I think the hallucinations are due to stress."

"And the weather... it's getting worse," Elena interjected. "We're completely cut off. No communication, no way out. We're trapped here. It's as if the relic is trying to isolate us, and it has done a good job of accomplishing that."

Captain Mitchell's expression grew grim. "Has anyone else experienced hallucinations?"

No one responded.

"We need a plan," Captain Mitchell continued. "First, we need to ensure everyone's safety. Dr. Warren, can we move the relic further away from the living quarters? Perhaps dig a hole and place it back in the ice."

Alice nodded. "I'll see to it, but we need to be careful. Prolonged exposure might start affecting us all."

Captain Mitchell sighed, the weight of the situation pressing down on him. "Alright. You and I will move it to the far end of the facility outside. Everyone else, stay in pairs. No one goes anywhere alone. If you experience anything unusual, report it immediately."

Suddenly, the lights flickered and a low, ominous hum filled the room. Everyone tensed, their eyes darting around nervously.

"What the hell is that?" a frightened team member asked.

"It's the relic. It's... reacting," Alice said, her alarm evident.

"Stay calm. We need to move it now," Captain Mitchell said firmly.

With flashlights in hand, Captain Mitchell and Alice braved the howling wind, making their way toward the containment building. The other team members watched from various windows, their faces pressed against the glass. Mitchell and Alice clung to ropes strung between the two buildings, the gale threatening to tear them away.

Reaching the containment building, the hum grew louder and more insistent, shadows flickering at the edges of their vision.

"Do you feel that? It's like... it's trying to get inside my head," Alice said, struggling to focus.

"Just keep moving. We need to get this thing as far away as possible," Captain Mitchell replied, gritting his teeth.

"Don't you feel it?" Alice insisted.

"No. For some reason, it is focused on you, but we don't have time to worry about that now. We need to get this thing outside," Mitchell said firmly. They secured the relic in a bag and headed toward the exit door.

"Here, let me carry it since it is not going after me," Captain Mitchell offered.

They started for the exit door. As Captain Mitchell opened it, the door slammed shut. He tried to open it again. “It must be the storm. You’ll need to hold the relic so I can force it open.”

As he turned to hand the relic to Alice, they both saw a distorted, shadowy figure standing there, its eyes glowing with an unnatural light.

“You cannot escape us. This place is ours now,” the figure whispered in a chilling voice.

“What is that? Is it real?” Alice asked, terrified.

“Back away slowly,” Captain Mitchell instructed, stepping forward. He pulled out his service weapon and fired two shots into the figure. The figure lunged forward, dissolving into a swarm of dark, spectral forms that enveloped the corridor. Screams echoed as the shadows passed through them, leaving icy, burning pain in their wake.

Alice screamed, brushing off the shadows. Captain Mitchell rushed to hold her as the Ice Phantom vanished. He grabbed the relic and forced the door open. “Well, at least you are no longer the only one seeing hallucinations,” a smiling Mitchell said.

Captain Mitchell and Alice struggled through the worsening weather, carrying the relic. The wind howled, and the snow swirled around them as they fought their way to a spot a short distance from the building. They began digging frantically.

“Hurry, we don’t have much time,” Alice urged, shivering from the cold. They buried the relic, covering it with as much snow and ice as they could. The eerie glow faded as they finished.

"Let's get back inside," Captain Mitchell panted, exhausted.

The team regrouped in the main research building, huddled around a table. Captain Mitchell and Alice, covered in snow and visibly shaken, recounted the events.

"Did burying it work?" Dr. Lee asked, his concern evident.

"For now. But we're not out of the woods yet. We need to figure out what we're dealing with and how to stop it permanently," Captain Mitchell replied, tired but resolute.

"And where the creature who made those footprints ended up. It has to be out there somewhere," D. Lee added.

Alice nodded. "The relic seems to be connected to these... entities. We need to study it further, but from a safe distance. Maybe there's something in our data that can help us understand its origin and purpose."

Elena looked confused. "What do you mean by entities?"

"I experienced a hallucination at the same time as Dr. Warren," Captain Mitchell explained. "I fired several rounds into it, but the phantom or whatever it was disappeared."

"And if those things come back, we need to be prepared," said one of the team members. "We'll set up a perimeter and keep watch in shifts."

"What if burying it just made things worse?" another team member asked, their voice shaking.

"We'll deal with it as it comes," Captain Mitchell said, his voice steadfast. "Right now, we need to stay calm, stay together, and stay vigilant. This isn't over, but we're not giving up."

CHAPTER 5

From the safety of the main research building, the team peered out at the faint glow emanating from beneath the ice where the relic lay buried. The low, pulsing sound resonated through the walls, sending chills down their spines.

Alice, her face etched with concern, broke the silence. "Do you hear that? The relic... it's still active."

Captain Mitchell, equally uneasy, nodded. "Stay focused. We need answers, and fast. Keep monitoring the area and report any changes immediately. Gather your weapons and let's meet in the cafeteria. We need to eat and build up our strength."

The team dispersed, gathering weapons and equipment, preparing for the unknown horrors that lay ahead. The wind howled outside, carrying with it the whispers of the unseen entities—a haunting reminder that the nightmare was far from over.

"Let's move to the dining room," Captain Mitchell instructed the team.

Most of the team gathered in the cafeteria, armed and on edge. Captain Mitchell stood at the head of the table, trying to project calm and authority.

"Alright, everyone," he began. "We need to piece together how this all started. Maybe understanding the sequence of events will give us some clues on how to deal with this."

Alice nodded. "We should start from the beginning. Elena, you first noticed the radio waves, right?"

Elena took a deep breath. "Yes. About a week ago, I picked up an unusual frequency on the radio. It was faint, but it was there. I tracked it to the north, towards the glacier."

Dr. Lee leaned forward. "And that's when we decided to investigate. We thought it might be a natural phenomenon, or at least something explainable."

Alice interjected, "We took the snowmobiles and followed the signal. The further we went, the stronger the signal became. Until we found the tracks in the snow."

A team member nodded in agreement. "Yeah, those tracks... they weren't human. Too big, too deep. And they led us to that impact site."

Alice continued, "We found the remains of the alien ship which were scattered across the ice. It was clear that it had been there for a long time, buried under the snow. That's when we found the relic and noticed footprints leading away from the crash site. I remember touching the block of ice trying to get a better look at the object. The moment I did, I felt… something. Like a surge of energy. The hallucinations started once I got back here."

A team member interrupted her. "But why didn't the relic affect us right after the crash? And, why does it create hallucinations to just you and Captain Mitchell?"

Alice looked thoughtful. "All good questions. Maybe the relic was dormant until we disturbed it. Or perhaps it's reacting to our presence, feeding off our fear and emotions."

Captain Mitchell, resolute, replied, "Whatever the case, we need to figure out how to neutralize it. Understanding its origin and purpose is our best shot. We need to keep our heads and work together."

Alice nodded. "Agreed. We should go through our data, see if there's anything we missed. Any patterns or clues that could help us."

"Did radar pick up the craft before it crashed?" Dr. Lee asked.

"No, nothing on radar. Only the sudden frequency pulse," Alice answered.

Elena stood up. "I'll start analyzing the radio waves again. Maybe there's something in the signal that we overlooked."

Captain Mitchell nodded. "Good. The rest of you, keep a close watch. Report any changes, no matter how small. And stay armed. We don't know what else might be out there."

Dr. Lee raised a hand. "I'd like to make an additional proposal. We need to re-examine the crash site after the storm. Hopefully, some of the craft will still be visible, and we can attempt to determine the direction the occupant took."

Everyone glanced at each other and then focused on Captain Mitchell.

"Let's table that idea until we get through this storm," Captain Mitchell decided.

The team dispersed, each member taking on their assigned tasks. The atmosphere was tense, but there was a renewed sense of purpose. Outside, the glow beneath the ice pulsed ominously, a constant reminder of the lurking danger.

The next morning dawned uneventfully. Captain Mitchell gathered the team in the dining hall and addressed them.

"I've considered Dr. Lee's motion to reinvestigate the crash site," Captain Mitchell began. "Elena has reported that we will have a four-hour window of opportunity with the storm, but we must return quickly before the main thrust hits us." The team nodded in agreement and began preparing to head out.

As they approached the crash site, the wind picked up, howling through the trees, and visibility started to decrease. The snow crunched under their boots, creating an eerie silence between the gusts of wind.

"Stay close, everyone. We don't have much time," Captain Mitchell instructed.

At the crash site, they found very little due to the freshly fallen snow. No footprints were visible, but Alice pointed in the direction where she last saw them. "This is where the footprints were last visible before the snow covered them," Dr. Warren said.

Suddenly, a distant noise caught their attention, sounding like metal scraping against metal. The team froze, exchanging worried glances.

"Did you hear that?" Dr. Lee asked, his voice tense.

"Stay alert. It could be anything," Captain Mitchell replied. The wind intensified, and the sound grew louder, echoing through the snowy landscape. They inched forward cautiously, hearts pounding.

"We should keep going. There might be more clues just ahead," Dr. Lee urged.

"Dr. Lee, we have to stick to the plan. The storm window is closing fast," Captain Mitchell reminded him. Reluctantly, they started to retreat, the mysterious noise still lingering in the air.

As they returned to the research facility, Dr. Lee was visibly upset, wanting to continue further in the direction of the former footprints. "We should have gone further. We might have found something important," Dr. Lee insisted.

Captain Mitchell placed a reassuring hand on his shoulder. "I understand your frustration, Dr. Lee, but we can't risk getting caught in the storm. We'll reassess our approach once it passes."

Alice nodded in agreement. "Captain's right. Safety first. We'll get another chance."

Dr. Lee sighed, his eyes still holding a glimmer of determination. "I just hope we don't miss something crucial." The team made their way back inside, the wind howling behind them as the storm began to intensify.

The team was back at the research facility, the wind howling outside as the storm intensified. "Alright, everyone, stay vigilant. The storm is getting worse, and we need to be prepared for anything," Captain Mitchell instructed. The team nodded and dispersed to their duties.

In the containment building, two security team members, Jenkins and Davis, stood guard at an access point. Jenkins, a twenty-something black man, peered out into the swirling snow. "I hate this weather. Gives me the creeps," he shouted to Davis, a twenty-something Asian man. "I mean, I didn't sign up for some alien shit. Just wanted to put in my twenty and retire on some Caribbean Island."

"Yeah, I know. The whole crash site scared the shit out of me. And then, when Dr. Warren talked about the footprints and pointed to the last known directions of its' footprints, damn…..Just stay focused. Captain wants us on high alert," Davis replied.

Suddenly, a loud thud echoed against the side of the building as if something had crashed against it. Both guards jumped, exchanging wary glances.

"Did you hear that?" Jenkins asked, his voice tense.

"Yeah, stay sharp," Davis responded. Another thud, louder this time, followed by the sound of scraping metal. Jenkins raised his flashlight, pointing it toward the noise, trying to pierce the darkness and swirling snow. "Sounds like something is outside and trying to see how to enter."

Jenkins squinted into the darkness. "What the hell is that?" Before Davis could respond, a massive shadow loomed outside the window. The glass shattered, and a grotesque, otherworldly creature burst through, snarling.

It stood over ten feet tall, solid and menacing, with eyes glowing a fiery red. Its skin was a sickly gray, covered in jagged scales and oozing sores. Long, sharp claws extended from its gnarled hands, and its mouth was filled with rows of needle-like teeth.

"Davis, get back!" Jenkins shouted, trying to raise his weapon. But it was too late. The creature lunged at Jenkins, its claws slashing through him. Blood sprayed on the walls. He fell to the ground, lifeless.

Davis fired his weapon, but the creature barely flinched. The bullets seemed to bounce off its tough hide, and it turned its fiery gaze toward him, advancing with a terrifying growl. He pushed the red alarm button on the wall. The alarm blared, and red lights flashed throughout the facility. The creature did not react to the light or sound. Captain Mitchell and the others rushed towards the containment building.

"What's happening? Report!" Captain Mitchell demanded.

"It's the creature! It's here!" Alice shouted.

Armed, they reached the containment building finding Davis, badly wounded, struggling to keep the creature at bay. Alice screamed seeing Davis hold his own intestines in his hands. The creature turned its attention towards them, eyes glowing menacingly. It shook it's lizard like head throw blood from its mouth. It claws still displaying remains of the two guards.

"Fall back! Secure the area!" Captain Mitchell ordered. The team retreated, but the creature grabbed Davis, dragging him through the broken window. His screams echoed as the team looked on in horror.

"We have to stop it! We can't let it get to the relic!" Dr. Lee urged.

"That's the last of our concerns," Captain Mitchell replied. "Everyone, grab what you can. We need to contain it before it reaches the main facility!" The team scrambled to gather their weapons and equipment, their minds racing with fear and determination. The creature's growls and Davis's fading screams spurred them into action, knowing the survival of the entire facility depended on their swift response.

CHAPTER 6

The night was eerily quiet inside the research facility's command center. The team, drenched in sweat and breathing heavily, regrouped with a sense of urgency. Captain Mitchell broke the silence, his voice steady despite the chaos around them.

"We need to come up with a plan. That thing is after the relic. If it gets inside, we're all dead," he said, his eyes scanning the anxious faces of his team.

Alice, her mind racing, offered a suggestion. "We have to lure it away from the building. Maybe we can trap it somehow."

"But how?" Dr. Lee interjected, frustration and fear evident in his tone. "It's too strong and fast."

Captain Mitchell nodded, already formulating a strategy. "We'll use the emergency lockdown system. Seal off sections of the facility to contain its movements. Dr. Warren, get to the secondary control room and start the lockdown sequence. The rest of us will try to distract it."

Alice's face was set with determination. "Got it. Be careful, everyone."

The team split up, each member acutely aware of the danger that lay ahead. As they approached the containment building, the tension in the air was palpable. The creature's roar echoed through the corridors, a bone-chilling sound that sent shivers down their spines.

"He's trying to return to the containment building." Captain Mitchell raised his weapon, firing a shot to get the creature's attention. "Hey! Over here, you ugly bastard!" he shouted, his voice cutting through the noise.

The creature turned, its eyes locking onto Mitchell. With a snarl, it charged towards them. Dr. Lee and the others threw objects and fired their weapons, doing everything they could to draw it away from the containment building.

"I think he is probing us. Not only is it looking for a way to return to the building, but it is testing our fire power," Captain Mitchell shouted.

"It's working! Keep moving!" Dr. Lee yelled, his heart pounding in his chest.

Meanwhile, in the control room, Alice frantically typed at the control panel, initiating the lockdown sequence. Her fingers flew over the keys, and metal shutters began to descend, sectioning off parts of the facility. She watched the progress on the screen, willing the system to move faster.

"Come on, come on..." she muttered under her breath, the weight of the situation pressing down on her.

The creature crashed violently into a sealed-off section of the containment building, thrashing wildly as it tried to break free. The metal barriers held for now, but Captain Tom Mitchell knew their respite was temporary.

"We've got it contained for now, but we need a permanent solution," he said, his voice tense.

Dr. Lee, still catching his breath, nodded. "We have to find a way to neutralize it. Maybe something in the relic can help us understand its weaknesses."

Captain Mitchell's eyes narrowed in thought. "Alright, let's regroup and figure out our next move. I have an idea. Stay alert."

In the command center, the team huddled together, exhaustion evident on their faces. The containment building's metal shutters held firm, but the creature's roars and thrashing echoed ominously through the video monitor.

Captain Mitchell broke the uneasy silence. "Alright, we've got it contained for now, but we need a way to neutralize it permanently."

Alice frowned. "Its resilience is unlike anything we've seen. Bullets barely slow it down."

"We need to find its weakness, and fast," Dr. Lee added, urgency in his voice.

Mitchell nodded thoughtfully. "Maybe we're approaching this the wrong way. Bullets aren't working, but what about electricity?"

Dr. Silva raised an eyebrow. "Electricity? You think it could be vulnerable to high voltage?"

"It's worth a shot," Captain Mitchell replied. "A creature like that, with its biological makeup, might not handle an electrical current well. We have tasers and the electrical equipment in the lab. We can rig something up."

Dr. Silva nodded, considering the plan. "It's risky, but we don't have many options. If we can incapacitate it long enough, maybe we can find a more permanent solution."

A team member stepped forward. "I'll need access to the lab's power grid. We can rig some high-voltage conductors to act as makeshift weapons."

"Good," Captain Mitchell said, his voice firm. "Everyone, listen up. Dr. Warren and I will work on the electrical setup. The rest of you, gather any tasers, stun guns, and high-voltage equipment you can find. We need to move fast before it breaks through."

The team nodded in unison, springing into action. They scattered through the facility, gathering equipment and heading to the lab, their minds focused on the urgent task at hand. The clock was ticking, and they had to act before the creature found a way to escape its temporary prison.

Alice and Captain Tom Mitchell worked with feverish intensity in the lab, their hands moving quickly to set up makeshift electrical weapons. They connected the devices to portable power sources, their minds laser-focused on the task at hand.

"We'll need to get close enough to use these," Alice said, glancing up at Mitchell. "The risk is high, but it's our best chance."

Captain Mitchell nodded, his face grim but determined. "I know. We'll coordinate our attack and hit it with everything we've got."

Armed with their newly rigged electrical weapons, the team made their way to the containment building. The creature's roars and violent thrashing reverberated through the metal walls, a constant reminder of the imminent danger. The tension was palpable as they approached, each step bringing them closer to the terrifying confrontation that awaited.

Captain Mitchell looked back at his team, his eyes filled with resolve. "Stay focused and stick to the plan. We hit it hard and fast. Let's move." The team positioned themselves around the containment building's entrance, nerves taut with anticipation.

"Now!" Captain Mitchell commanded. They burst in, weapons ready. The creature turned, snarling, its eyes glowing with rage. The team unleashed a barrage of electrical currents. The creature screeched in pain, convulsing as the electricity coursed through its body.

"It's working! Keep going!" Dr. Lee yelled, hope sparking in his voice. The creature thrashed wildly but began to weaken, its movements becoming sluggish.

"Don't let up! We're almost there!" Mitchell urged. Finally, the creature collapsed, incapacitated by the electrical assault. Its body twitches a few times and then stops. The team maintains a safe distance, breathing heavily, the air filled with the sharp smell of ozone.

Alice exhaled deeply. "We did it. It's down, but we need to act fast. This might not last long."

"Secure it and get ready for phase two," Mitchell ordered. "We need to figure out how to contain it permanently before it regains strength." As the team celebrated, exchanging relieved smiles, Dr. Silva cautiously approached the creature. A low growl rumbled from its throat, and its eyes snapped open, glowing fiercely.

"Oh no, it's waking up!" Dr. Silva shouted, panic creeping into his voice. Before anyone could react, the creature surged to its feet, roaring in fury. It smashed through a nearby window with terrifying strength, sending shards of glass flying everywhere.

"It's escaping! After it!" Mitchell yelled, rallying the team into action once more.

Outside the containment building, the team scrambled to chase the creature as it disappeared into the darkness, its roars echoing through the night. The storm raged on, making the pursuit even more perilous.

Alice's voice cut through the chaos. "We can't let it get away. Who knows what it'll do out there!"

Captain Mitchell quickly assessed the situation. "No! Wait. Everyone needs to return to the facility. If we try to track it down in this blizzard, we're playing into its hands. Back to the facility now!"

Reluctantly, the team heeded Captain Mitchell's command, retreating back to the safety of the research facility, the storm's fury swallowing the sounds of their retreat.

CHAPTER 7

The dining room was filled with a palpable tension as everyone glanced at each other, fear evident in their eyes. Captain Mitchell sensed the unease and broke the silence with a wry smile.

"Well, we kicked its ass for a little while," he said, attempting to lighten the mood. The team responded with nervous laughter, the tension easing slightly.

"We need to get a hot meal in us and come up with a different strategy. What do you all say?" Mitchell continued. Without waiting for an answer, everyone began making themselves something to eat and drink, the mundane task a brief respite from the chaos.

Later, as they ate and tried to regain their strength, the atmosphere remained tense but calm. Dr. Lee approached Alice, who was sitting alone at a table, deep in thought.

"Alice, can I talk to you for a second?" Dr. Lee asked, his voice soft.

"Sure, Marcus. What's on your mind?" she replied, looking up.

"I can't help but feel that we're missing out on a great opportunity here," he said, his tone earnest.

"What do you mean?" Alice asked, curiosity piqued.

"You're a xenobiologist. This creature is unlike anything we've ever encountered. We should be trying to capture it, study it, understand its biology and origins," Dr. Lee explained.

Alice sighed. "I understand that, Marcus. But it's dangerous. It already killed Jenkins and wounded Davis. We can't risk any more lives."

"I know it's risky but think about the potential discoveries. This could change everything we know about extraterrestrial life. Isn't that worth the risk?" Dr. Lee pressed.

"Of course, it's worth it. But we need to be smart about it. We can't just rush in blindly," Alice replied, her voice firm.

"I'm not suggesting we be reckless. But we have to consider the bigger picture. This creature could hold the key to so many questions we've had for years. And you, of all people, should be leading that charge," Dr. Lee insisted.

Alice's eyes flashed with anger. "Marcus, it's not just about the science. This thing has already killed one of our team members. We can't afford to lose anyone else. It has to be destroyed."

"But Alice, think of what we could learn. We owe it to ourselves and to science to at least try to capture it," Dr. Lee argued.

"And risk more lives? No, Marcus. My responsibility is to this team. We destroy it, and we ensure everyone here stays alive," Alice said, her voice rising.

"This is a once-in-a-lifetime opportunity. We might never get another chance like this," Dr. Lee pleaded.

"I get that, but we're not equipped to handle this safely. The priority is to protect everyone here. That means neutralizing the threat," Alice responded, her tone final.

"I can't believe you're saying this," Dr. Lee said, frustration evident.

"I don't like it any more than you do, but it's the reality we're facing," Alice said, her voice softening. Alice and Dr. Lee approached Captain Mitchell, who was in deep discussion with the team about their next steps.

"Captain, we need to talk," Alice said, her voice steady. "Marcus and I have been discussing our next move."

"I'm listening," Captain Mitchell replied, turning his attention to them.

"We should try to capture the creature," Dr. Lee began. "The scientific implications are too great to ignore."

"No, Captain," Alice interjected firmly. "This thing has already killed two of our team members. It's too dangerous. We need to destroy it before it kills again."

Captain Mitchell nodded, understanding the weight of both arguments. "I understand both sides, but we can't afford to lose any more people, Dr. Lee. Safety comes first. We need to find a way to neutralize this creature once and for all."

"This is a mistake," Dr. Lee argued. "We're letting fear dictate our actions."

"We're letting common sense and survival dictate our actions," Alice shot back. "It has to be done."

Captain Mitchell raised his voice to address the whole team. "Listen up, everyone. What we've learned so far is that the creature is only stunned when we use conventional weapons. When we hit it with electricity, it was temporarily incapacitated but quickly revived. Frankly, I'm out of ideas."

He glanced around the room, hoping for some input.

"We need to think outside the box," Alice suggested. "Maybe there's something we haven't tried yet."

"What about using higher voltage?" Dr. Silva proposed. "Something more powerful than what we've used so far? Enough to really knock it out."

"That could work," Captain Mitchell acknowledged, "but we need to be sure we can handle it safely. Any other ideas?"

"We could try a combination of methods," Alice added. "Hit it with high voltage and then contain it somehow."

A team member spoke up, "What about good old fire?"

A buzz broke out among the team members as they considered the suggestion, the tension slowly giving way to a cautious optimism as they brainstormed potential solutions.

Alice spoke up, her mind racing with possibilities. "Fire? It could work. Many creatures have vulnerabilities to high heat. We haven't tried that yet."

Dr. Lee nodded, considering the idea. "It's a possibility. But how do we control it without burning down the facility?"

Captain Mitchell jumped in with a suggestion. "We could use portable flamethrowers or set a controlled fire trap. We need to think of a way to direct the fire at the creature without endangering ourselves or the structure."

"Maybe we can lure it into an area where we've set up controlled burn points," Dr. Lee proposed. "Use barriers to contain the fire to that specific area and have some security personnel carry fire extinguishers."

Alice agreed, though her tone was cautious. "It's risky, but it might be our best shot. We'll need to be precise and like Dr. Lee said, ensure we have fire suppression ready in case it gets out of hand."

"Alright," Captain Mitchell said, taking charge. "Let's gather all the fire-based equipment we have and start planning this out. We'll set up a trap and lure the creature in. But remember, safety first. If anything goes wrong, we switch to Plan B and destroy it by any means necessary."

The team nodded in agreement, feeling a renewed sense of determination as they began to strategize their next move. Amidst the planning, Elena began showing symptoms of the flu: coughing, a runny nose, and a fever. The team would need to act quickly, not only to stop the creature but also to address this new concern.

"Elena, come with me to the sick bay," Dr. Silva instructed, concern etched on his face. Dr. Silva guided Elena to a chair. "Sit here, Elena, and unbutton your blouse. How long have you had this cough?"

Elena sighed, feeling the weight of her fatigue. "A few days, I guess. I wasn't keeping track of it. The cough keeps me awake at night." Dr. Silva placed his stethoscope on various parts of Elena's chest, listening intently as she coughed a few times. He examined her throat before stepping back with a prognosis.

"I think, young lady, you have a bout of the flu. No more venturing outside unless you want to develop pneumonia. Rest, stay warm, and get some soup in the kitchen. Also, drink a lot of liquids. Got it?"

"Yes, Doctor," Elena replied, buttoning up her blouse. She left the sick bay, feeling a mix of relief and concern as she headed back to the team.

The creature attacked again, bursting through a wall of the adjacent hallway with terrifying force. The team, armed with flamethrowers, quickly moved into position. "Everyone ready? On my signal!" Captain Mitchell commanded, his voice steady. The creature roared and charged towards them, its eyes blazing with fury.

"Now!" Captain Mitchell shouted.

The team unleashed a wall of fire, directing the flames at the creature. It screeched in pain, thrashing violently as the heat overwhelmed it. "It's working! Keep it up!" Dr. Lee encouraged, his voice rising above the chaos. Despite the flames, the creature showed signs of resilience, slowly pushing through the inferno. The team intensified their efforts, determined to contain the beast.

"It's getting through! We need to fall back!" Alice shouted, urgency in her voice. The creature broke free, escaping through the hole in the wall it had entered from, disappearing into the darkness once more. The team watched, frustrated but undeterred.

"Why do you think it continues to return?" Dr. Lee asked, perplexed. "If it's picking up signals from the relic, why wouldn't it be outside digging it up?"

"I wish I had answers for you, doctor, but I don't," Captain Mitchell replied, shaking his head.

"If I may," Dr. Silva said, getting everyone's attention. "We never questioned why, when the creature killed the two security team members, he took both of their bodies with them. I mean, it was under attack from us, yet it was determined to take their corpses when it retreated."

Alice pondered for a moment. "I think it's coming back here because we are its food source. I'm not sure yet why it's not searching for the relic."

As they discussed the creature's behavior, Elena continued to sneeze, wiping her nose and coughing. Dr. Frank Silva turned to her sympathetically.

"Wish I could give you something, but it's a virus," he said.

"I'll be fine," Elena responded.

A team member spoke up, adding a new perspective. "Maybe it's not just the relic or us. What if it's attracted to the energy we're generating? All our equipment, the containment field—it could be drawing it in."

Dr. Silva nodded thoughtfully. "That's a good point. Many creatures are attracted to certain energy frequencies. The relic might have started it, but our own energy output could be keeping it here."

Dr. Lee's eyes widened with realization. "And if it's after energy, that could explain why it seems to be getting stronger. It's feeding off our power sources."

The team absorbed this new theory, understanding they needed to adjust their strategy to not only combat the creature but also address the energy sources that might be attracting it.

CHAPTER 8

"But why attack us directly?" Alice questioned. "If it's just after energy, why not go straight for the generators?"

A team member offered a theory. "It could be territorial. We're in its perceived domain, and it's trying to eliminate us as threats, or Dr. Warren, as you suggested, it has two objectives, food, and energy."

"Or it might see us as an easy energy source," Dr. Lee added. "I agree, young man. If it consumes biological energy as well, we could be a dual-purpose target—both food and energy."

Captain Mitchell considered their words. "So, we have a creature that's drawn to both biological and electronic energy. We need to figure out how to cut off its access to these sources without compromising our safety."

"Maybe we should consider shutting down some of our non-essential systems," Dr. Lee suggested.

"Reduce our energy footprint and see if that has any effect."

"That's a start," Alice agreed, "but we also need to prepare for its return. We can't rely on cutting off its energy alone. We need to be ready to neutralize it when it comes back."

"I'll start re-routing power to essential systems only," another team member volunteered. "If we can make this place less attractive, maybe we can buy some time."

"And I'll check our generator defenses," said another. "If it tries to go for our power, we need to be ready to protect those sources."

The team nodded in agreement, feeling a renewed sense of purpose as they split up to implement their new strategies. The clock was ticking, and they knew the creature would return soon. They had to be ready.

The team huddled around a table, weapons at the ready. The atmosphere was heavy with fear and uncertainty. Alice and Dr. Silva were deep in discussion, trying to formulate their next steps.

"We need to figure out what's causing these hallucinations," Alice said, her voice tense. "The relic must be emitting some kind of frequency that's affecting our minds."

Suddenly, Team Member #2 began looking around frantically. "Look out! It's coming!" he shouted, pulling out his weapon and firing several shots wildly. The bullets whizzed past Alice and Dr. Silva, the sound of gunfire echoing through the room and causing everyone to jump and grab their weapons.

"Stop firing! Holster your weapon!" Captain Mitchell commanded, his voice cutting through the chaos.

Dr. Silva turned to Team Member #2, his face pale with shock. "What the hell are you doing? There's nothing there!"

Breathing heavily, eyes wide with fear, Team Member #2 lowered his weapon. "I... I saw it. It was right there," he stammered.

Alice's expression was grim. "This is exactly what I'm talking about. The relic is buried out there in the snow, but it's still affecting us. We need to contain this before someone gets seriously hurt."

Captain Mitchell addressed the team, his tone firm. "Everyone, listen up. We need to stay calm and stick together. No more shooting unless there's a clear threat. Understood?" The team nodded, visibly shaken but trying to regain their composure, the reality of their situation weighing heavily on their minds.

"We need to run more tests, but first, we have to secure the area," Alice said, urgency in her voice. "The hallucinations are only going to get worse if we don't find a way to shield ourselves from the relic's influence."

Dr. Silva nodded. "We can set up a perimeter and use the equipment we have to monitor for any unusual frequencies. Maybe we can find a way to block it."

"Alright, let's move," Captain Mitchell instructed. "Stay alert and keep your wits about you. We'll get through this." The team began to mobilize, checking their gear and preparing to head out into the frigid night. The tension was palpable as they stepped out of the relative safety of the building and into the dark, snow-covered landscape.

Before they left, Dr. Silva walked over to Elena. "You are not going outside, Elena," he said firmly, touching her forehead. "Your fever is higher."

"I can't stay in my quarters. What if the creature gets in?" Elena protested.

"You need to rest, but I understand," Dr. Silva said, his voice softening. "Stay with the others until we return." Elena nodded reluctantly, and the team stepped into the biting cold, ready to face the unknown challenges that awaited them in the darkness.

The wind howled as Dr. Lee, Alice, Captain Mitchell, and two security members stepped outside into the frigid night. The snow crunched under their boots, visibility low in the swirling snowstorm. They moved with purpose, acutely aware of the danger lurking in the darkness.

"We need to move quickly," Dr. Lee shouted over the wind. "The longer we're out here, the more vulnerable we are."

"Stay alert and keep your weapons ready," Captain Mitchell warned. "We don't know where that thing is." They reached the spot where they had buried the relic. The team formed a defensive perimeter while Dr. Warren and Dr. Lee started digging, shoveling snow with frantic urgency.

"We have to be careful," Dr. Warren said cautiously. "If the relic is affecting us, we need to minimize exposure."

"Almost there. Just a little more," Dr. Lee replied, determined. Finally, they uncovered the relic, its ominous glow piercing through the snow. Alice and Dr. Lee carefully lifted it out, wrapping it in a protective cover.

"Alright, let's move. Keep tight formation," Captain Mitchell ordered.They started their trek back to the containment building, the tension palpable. Every shadow, every gust of wind felt like a potential threat.

Suddenly, a horrifying roar pierced the night. The creature burst from the snow, a monstrous silhouette against the icy backdrop. It lunged at the team with terrifying speed.

"It's here! Open fire!" screamed one of the security team members. The team unleashed a barrage of gunfire, but the creature was relentless. Flamethrowers seemed to slow it down, but it swiped at the security team member, its massive claws tearing into him. Blood sprayed across the snow as he screamed in agony.

"Fall back! Fall back!" Captain Mitchell yelled. The creature grabbed the security team member, dragging him off into the darkness. His screams faded into the howling wind.

"We have to go! Now!" Captain Mitchell ordered, his voice rapid and urgent. They kept shooting, but the creature disappeared, leaving only blood and chaos in its wake. Shaken and terrified, the team resumed their retreat to the containment building, the relic clutched tightly in Alice's arms.

"We can't let it happen again. Everyone inside, now!" Captain Mitchell commanded as they hurried back into the relative safety of the building.

CHAPTER 9

Night had fallen as they rushed into the containment building, slamming the door shut behind them. The harsh reality of their situation settled in as they caught their breath. "We need to find a way to stop that thing," Dr. Lee panted. "It's not just the relic; it's something more."

Captain Mitchell, with steely resolve, replied, "We will. But first, we secure this damn relic." The team regrouped, their fear transforming into determination. The battle was far from over. They watched as Alice carefully placed the relic in a metal box.

"Perhaps this metal can contain whatever this thing is emanating," Dr. Warren said hopefully. She then looked at Captain Mitchell and noticed he didn't look well. "Tom, do you feel okay? You look like you're running a fever."

"Probably picked up the bug from Elena," Captain Mitchell replied. "I'll check with Dr. Silva when we get back to the main building. Let's get out of here. We can return later after the sun comes up."

Upon returning to the main facility, Dr. Warren sought out Dr. Silva to check on Captain Mitchell. "Does anyone know where Dr. Silva is?" she asked urgently.

Elena, looking concerned, responded, "The last time I saw him, he was in his office. While you were gone, he found some liquid left behind by the creature. It must have cut itself either gaining access or when it fled." Dr. Warren nodded, the new information sparking a glimmer of hope. She headed towards Dr. Silva's office, determined to find answers and ensure Captain Mitchell received the care he needed.

Captain Mitchell and Alice entered the sick bay, finding Dr. Silva bent over a microscope. He looked up when he heard them enter. "I have another sick one for you," Alice said, nodding towards Mitchell.

Dr. Silva motioned for Captain Mitchell to take a seat and began examining him. "Yep. Another case of the flu," he confirmed. "You can thank Elena when you see her. Nothing I can do for you, Captain, except recommend rest, fluids, and staying warm. Just have to let the virus run its course and avoid pneumonia. How did you do with the relic?"

"It's secured in a metal box in the containment building," Captain Mitchell replied. "Not sure if that's going to help or not but reburying it in the snow did nothing."

Dr. Warren interjected, "I understand you found some liquid left behind by the creature."

Dr. Silva nodded and returned to his microscope, examining the blood sample while Alice and Captain Mitchell looked on, hopeful that this discovery might provide new insights.

Dr. Silva peered into the microscope, amazement in his voice. "This is incredible. The creature's blood cells are... different. It appears to have both male and female reproductive cells."

Captain Mitchell's eyes widened. "You mean it can reproduce on its own?"

"Yes," Dr. Silva said solemnly. "It's hermaphroditic. If it reproduces, we could be dealing with more than one of these things soon."

"We need to find a way to stop it before that happens," Dr. Warren said, determination in her voice. Just then, Alice began to cough.

Dr. Silva glanced at her and shook his head. "No need to examine you, Alice. You're coming down with the flu too. Whatever strain this is, it spreads easily."

In the main research building, the team sat around a table, tension thick in the air. Dr. Warren, sniffling, took a seat next to Dr. Lee. "Remember when we first got here?" Dr. Lee said, trying to lighten the mood. "We were so excited to make groundbreaking discoveries."

"Yeah, those were simpler times," Alice replied with a weak smile. "Who would've thought we'd end up fighting for our lives against an alien creature?"

Captain Mitchell joined in, "I still remember my first mission. Thought I'd seen it all. Guess I was wrong." He gazed out of the frosted window, the swirling snowstorm outside a reflection of the chaos within their minds. The eerie silence of the Arctic night was broken only by the occasional howling wind and the distant, haunting echo of the creature's presence. Each team member had their own stories, their own nightmares that brought them to this frozen hell, but nothing could have prepared them for this.

Alice nodded, her eyes filled with a mixture of determination and fear. "We came here to uncover secrets, but it feels like we've awakened something that was never meant to be found. The hallucinations, the attacks... it's like the relic has a will of its own." The two, lost in thought, forgot about Dr. Silva's examination.

Dr. Silva, excitement creeping into his voice, interrupted, "Look at this, Alice. The creature's cells regenerate at an alarming rate. This could explain its resilience."

"If we could find a way to disrupt its cellular regeneration, we might have a chance to stop it," Dr. Warren suggested weakly.

Dr. Silva nodded. "We need more samples. We have to understand its biology better." The team, now united by a common purpose, began to discuss strategies for obtaining more samples and finding a way to stop the creature once and for all.

The team ventured outside again, this time to gather more samples of the creature from the jagged remains of the building facade. The wind howled as they moved cautiously, weapons drawn.

"Stay sharp. It could be anywhere," Smith said, scanning the area. Suddenly, the creature appeared, roaring as it charged. The team opened fire, but the creature seemed unfazed. It swiped at a security team member, sending him flying and then went over to retrieve the body before retreating in the frozen tundra.

"Fall back! Get inside!" Captain Mitchell shouted, firing his weapon.

"Wait! Look," Alice pointed out. "The creature has left a trail of its blood or whatever. We need to gather those samples."

"Okay, but quickly," Captain Mitchell agreed. The team retreated after collecting several vials of the creature's blood.

Making it safely back in the lab, Dr. Silva examined the new samples, his expression one of intense concentration. "There has to be something..." he muttered to himself.

"Doctor, can I take a look?" Elena asked, coughing.

"Be my guest. Maybe you can see something I can't," Dr. Silva replied. Elena peered through the microscope, observing the various cells moving and replicating. As she continued to cough and wipe her nose, she noticed a reaction in the blood cells. Their movement seemed to be slowing down.

"Doctor, look at this," she said, her voice filled with sudden excitement. "The cells are reacting to something in my mucus. It's slowing them down."

Dr. Silva's eyes widened as he leaned in to observe. "This could be it. We might have found the key to stopping this creature." Dr. Silva leaned in to look, his expression shifting to one of sudden understanding. "Of course! The virus is attacking the cells. We might be able to use it against the creature."

CHAPTER 10

As dusk approached, the team gathered again in the main building common area, this time with a new plan. Captain Mitchell addressed them, determination in his eyes. "Dr. Silva has discovered that the creature's cells react to the virus many of us now carry in our systems. We might be able to use it to our advantage."

Dr. Silva stepped forward to explain. "If we can create an aerosol compound of the flu virus, we might be able to disrupt the creature's regeneration. In high enough concentration, we could weaken or even kill it."

In the lab Dr. Silva, assisted by Alice and Dr. Lee, began isolating the virus from blood samples taken from Alice, Elena, and Captain Mitchell. The wind howled as they worked quickly, knowing the creature could attack at any moment. The long night was not disturbed by the creature.

Most of the team members had gathered in the dining room area for breakfast. Suddenly, Security Team Member #3 jumped up and pointed a gun at Security Team Member #4.

"What are you doing? I saw you talking to it," Team Member #3 shouted.

"What are you fucking talking about? Put the gun down!" Team Member #4 replied, confused.

Hearing the commotion, Alice and Captain Mitchell ran to the dining area. "Everyone, calm down! We're all on edge," Alice interjected.

"Holster that weapon! This isn't real. It's the relic. It's affecting our minds," Captain Mitchell ordered. As Team Member #3 holstered his weapon, another team member (#5) ran and tackled Team Member #6, strangling him until Captain Mitchell pushed him off.

"It's the creature! We have to kill it," Team Member #6 shouted, jumping back up to attack Team Member #3. Captain Mitchell slugged him, knocking him out.

"We need to neutralize the relic, and I mean now. The hallucinations are affecting everyone," Dr. Warren said urgently.

"You're right," Captain Mitchell agreed. "I think it's time to smash that object and be damned with science. Maybe after we neutralize it, engineers can put it back together without experiencing what we are going through." The team, now united with a clear objective, prepared to confront the relic and end its influence once and for all.

Everyone was startled by the sound of a wall crashing in the hallway off the dining room. They rushed to the scene the area with several team members armed with flamethrowers. When they arrived, the creature already had one arm inside. They all opened fire, the flames roaring as they engulfed the creature. It screamed and retreated back into the snow. Other team members quickly used fire extinguishers to put out the flames.

Dr. Alice Warren and Captain Tom Mitchell retreated to the command center where they stood over a table cluttered with maps, documents, and equipment. Both looked tense and exhausted. The room was dimly lit, with the flickering lights adding to the sense of urgency.

"We can't keep going like this. The hallucinations are getting worse and the creature seems to be increasing its attacks," Alice said, her voice filled with concern.

Captain Mitchell nodded. "I agree. We need to neutralize the source, and we need to do it now."

Dr. Warren took a deep breath. "That relic has to be destroyed. If we can get into the containment building, we can end this."

"We'll have to be fast and prepared for anything," Captain Mitchell replied grimly. "The creature might not give us another chance." Alice grabbed a heavy-duty flashlight and a toolkit. Captain Mitchell checked his weapon and grabbed a sledgehammer from a nearby rack.

Two security team members armed with flamethrowers followed. The team, resolved and ready, set out for the containment building, knowing this might be their last chance to end the nightmare.

Inside the containment building the air was thick with tension. Alice and Captain Mitchell moved cautiously through the darkened building, their flashlights cutting through the gloom. The containment building was eerily silent, the only sounds being their footsteps and the occasional creak of the structure.

They reached the chamber where the relic was still contained in a metal box. "Ready?" Captain Mitchell whispered.

Alice nodded, her voice shaky. "Ready." They approached the relic. Alice shook it out of the metal container onto a desk. Captain Mitchell raised a sledgehammer, his face set in determination.

Alice adjusted her grip on the flashlight, fully illuminating the relic. Suddenly, a loud crash echoed through the building, followed by the familiar, terrifying roar of the creature. They exchanged a look of urgency as security team members rushed toward the sound.

"Do it now!" Alice yelled.

"For everyone's sake!" Captain Mitchell raised the sledgehammer. With all his might, Captain Mitchell brought the sledgehammer down on the relic. It shattered, sending shards and a shockwave through the room. The glow faded instantly, and the oppressive feeling lifted.

"Did it work?" Alice asked, breathing heavily. The creature's roar faded, replaced by an eerie silence. They stood still, listening. They heard the creature's footstep in the snow as it retreated.

"He's run off again. I guess that did it," one of the security team members said.

"I think it did," Captain Mitchell said, his voice filled with relief. "Let's get back and see if the others are okay."

They turned and quickly made their way out of the containment building, their faces showing the strain and hope that this ordeal might finally be over. Alice glanced back at what was left of the relic, a sense of finality settling in.

Dr. Lee was alone in the laboratory, pacing back and forth. The dim light cast long shadows, and his frustration was evident. He stopped in front of a specimen jar, staring intently at a sample taken from the creature. The door creaked open and Alice Warren entered.

"Lee, we need to talk," Alice said gently.

Dr. Lee turned sharply. "About what, Alice? About how we're planning to destroy one of the most incredible discoveries in history?"

Alice sighed. "I understand how you feel, but this isn't just about science anymore. The creature is dangerous. It's already killed several people."

"And what if it's the key to unlocking unimaginable scientific advancements? Cures, new technologies—this creature could change everything!" Dr. Lee raised his voice.

"We can't take that risk. Our priority is the safety of everyone here. The hallucinations, the attacks—we're barely holding on," Alice replied firmly.

Stepping closer, more intense, Dr. Lee said, "Alice, we're scientists. We can't let fear dictate our actions. We need to understand this creature, not destroy it out of panic."

"Lee, it's not about panic. It's about survival. If we don't act, there won't be anyone left to study it," Alice said, her tone softening. Dr. Lee clenched his fists, struggling with the conflict between his scientific curiosity and the reality of the situation. He stared at the specimen jar, torn between the promise of discovery and the need to protect his team.

CHAPTER 11

Dr. Lee's expression turned bitter. "I just... I can't accept that. There has to be another way."

Alice reached out to him. "Maybe there is, but right now, we have to focus on the immediate threat. Help us find a solution that keeps everyone safe. We can't do this without you."

Dr. Lee looked down, his resolve wavering. Finally, he nodded, though reluctantly. "Alright, but I'm not giving up on finding a way to study it safely."

Alice smiled. "I wouldn't expect anything less from you."

The team, excluding Dr. Lee, gathered around the dining room table. Charts, diagrams, and notes were spread out. The atmosphere was tense but focused. "We need to find a way to lure the creature into a trap. Once it's contained, we can expose it to the virus," Captain Mitchell said.

"We know it's avoiding the areas where people are sick. Maybe we can use that to our advantage," Alice suggested.

Dr. Silva nodded. "We could set up a containment area and use some of the infected team's belongings as bait. The creature will likely steer clear of the virus."

"Right, and once it's in the trap, we flood the area with the virus. Dr. Silva, can you synthesize enough of it?" Captain Mitchell asked.

Dr. Silva looked concerned. "I can, but it will take some time. We need to make sure the dosage is high enough to be effective but safe for us."

"We need to act fast. Every moment we delay, we risk another attack," Dr. Warren urged.

The team continued to discuss logistics and strategies, their voices overlapping with urgency, as they worked to finalize their plan to trap and neutralize the creature.

Dr. Lee quietly slipped into the sick bay, glancing around to make sure no one was watching. The room was dimly lit, filled with medical equipment and supplies. Dr. Silva's workstation was cluttered with vials, notes, and samples.

Dr. Lee approached a refrigerated unit, opening it carefully. He scanned the labels on the vials, finally spotting one marked with the creature's blood. His hands shook slightly as he took the vial, slipping it into his lab coat pocket. "This could be the key..." he whispered to himself.

He quickly closed the unit and exited the sick bay, determined but wary. The scene shifted back to the dining room, where the team was still deep in discussion.

The team continued to debate their plan, unaware of Dr. Lee's secret mission. Their voices were filled with urgency and determination as they worked to finalize their strategy to trap and neutralize the creature.

"Alright, let's get to work. We don't have much time," Captain Mitchell said to the team.

"Tom, I have a thought," Alice interjected. "If you remember, when we hit the creature with electricity it stunned him to the point that we thought we had killed it."

"I remember. Go on," Captain Mitchell urged. The team gathered around a large table covered with maps, equipment, and notes. Alice, Captain Mitchell, Dr. Frank Silva, and the others were deep in discussion.

"Well, what if we can set up a situation where the creature enters an area we've wired with high voltage electricity?" Alice suggested, her voice serious and determined. "Once it enters that zone, we zap it, temporarily stunning it and allowing us to get close enough to really expose it to the virus."

Dr. Silva's eyes lit up with excitement. "That's a fantastic idea." The team exchanged determined looks, understanding the gravity of the situation and the slim chances of survival. They nodded in agreement.

"Alright, let's make this happen," Captain Mitchell said, almost shouting. "We need to work fast and coordinate our efforts perfectly."

Dr. Lee, though reluctant, voiced his concerns. "We should still consider the scientific implications of this creature. Killing it might not be the best course of action."

"Our priority is survival. We need to stop it before it kills us all," Dr. Silva responded firmly. The tension was palpable, but there was a sense of unity and determination as the team dispersed, each member heading to their tasks with purpose.

The team worked tirelessly, setting up high-voltage cables and positioning them around the designated zone. Each movement was deliberate, their focus intense as they prepared the trap.

In the control room Alice monitored the progress on multiple screens, coordinating with team members through a radio. "Keep the voltage steady," she instructed into the radio. "We need to make sure it's enough to stun but even better if it is killed."

"Understood. Everything is almost ready," Dr. Silva responded over the radio.

Night arrived and the team regrouped, tired but resolute. "This is it," Captain Mitchell said seriously. "Everyone knows their roles. Let's bring this creature down. Now we wait." They shared a final look of resolve before heading to their positions, prepared for the final showdown. The team gathered, waiting for the creature to attack. The tension in the air was almost unbearable.

"Alright, we need to stay sharp," Captain Mitchell said, looking around. "Let's set up shifts so everyone gets some rest. We can't afford to be exhausted when it comes."

The team members nodded in agreement as Captain Mitchell began assigning shifts. They settled in, the anticipation weighing heavily on them, knowing the creature could strike at any moment.

"Alice, you're with me on the first shift with half the security team," Captain Mitchell continued. "Dr. Silva, Dr. Lee, and the rest of you, get some sleep. We'll rotate in four hours." The team dispersed, finding spots to rest. Alice approached Captain Mitchell as he settled into a chair.

"You need rest too, you know," Alice said, sitting next to him. "Can't have our fearless leader collapsing on us."

Captain Mitchell smiled wearily. "Someone's got to keep an eye out."

"We'll get through this. We've faced worse odds before," Alice said, laying down next to him.

"I know. I trust this team. We'll make it," Captain Mitchell replied confidently. He stretched and turned to Alice. "What are you going to do when we get out of this fix we're in?"

"To tell you the truth, I haven't given it much thought. I didn't want to tell Dr. Lee, but most likely, the government will clamp a non-disclosure order on this whole incident. So there goes he and I being on the lecture circuit, describing the events we've gone through and how it all turns out. He, in my opinion, is a loose cannon. How about you?"

"God knows with the Air Force. Today, I'm freezing my ass off fighting a creature from outer space, and tomorrow I could be assigned to Hawaii exploring the effect of rusticles on the U.S.S. Arizona." Alice laughed. Silence took over for a short time between them.

"Alice, I know Steve death is still on your mind, but have you thought about getting married again?"

"Wow. Are you proposing, Tom?"

"And what if I am?" he answered rather sheepishly.

"You're serious, aren't you?" Alice asked, turning to face Tom directly.

"Well, yes. After we get out of here, I'll have over twenty-five years in, and frankly, I'm tired of being assigned all over this damn world. I think it's time to settle down. Find a nice home near a sandy beach where I can go fishing, parasailing, or just get a good sunburn."

"And you think you can handle me?" Alice said with a hint of flirtation.

Tom grinned. "Hell, I'm pretty good at giving orders."

Alice raised an eyebrow, a playful smirk forming on her lips. "Oh, really? Well, let me tell you, Tom, I'm not one to follow orders blindly. You might have your hands full."

"Hands full, huh?" Tom chuckled. "Well, I'm known for my multitasking skills. Think of it as a challenge."

Alice laughed, shaking her head. "A challenge, indeed. Just remember, I have a black belt in sarcasm and a Ph.D. in making life interesting."

Tom leaned in closer, his eyes sparkling with mischief. "Sounds like I've met my match. But hey, if I can face down a creature from outer space, I think I can handle you."

Alice smiled, feeling a warmth that had nothing to do with the freezing Arctic air. "You're on, Tom. Just don't say I didn't warn you." The embrace and share a passionate kiss.

As the night hung on, Dr. Lee sneaked into the storage room, looking around cautiously. He retrieved a vial containing the creature's blood and carefully hid it in a secure case, ready for transport. His resolve was clear—he wouldn't let this opportunity for scientific discovery slip away, no matter the cost.

The next morning, it became clear that the rotated shifts had helped. Everyone looked more rested but still anxious. The creature had not attacked. "Why hasn't it come yet? It should have attacked by now," Dr. Silva asked, frowning.

"Do you think it knows? Could it be aware of the trap?" Alice asked uneasily.

Captain Mitchell shook his head, doubtful. “How would it know? It can’t possibly...”

“What if it’s reading our minds?” Dr. Silva interrupted. “Remember how the relic created hallucinations. Perhaps it has the ability to do something similar. Or worse, what if it’s reproducing somewhere? Creating more of itself.” The team looked at each other, the weight of the new possibilities sinking in.

“We need to be prepared for anything,” Dr. Lee said quietly. “We can’t assume it will attack the way we expect.”

“Agreed,” Dr. Warren nodded. “We need to stay vigilant and adapt to whatever comes our way.” The team nodded in silent agreement, the tension in the room thick as they braced themselves for the unknown.

CHAPTER 12

The team was gathered, each member lost in their own thoughts. The tension was palpable, and the silence heavy. Elena, looking contemplative, broke the silence. "You know, there is something none of us addressed," she said. Everyone turned to look at Elena, curiosity and concern etched on their faces.

"We focused on the object we later called the relic after we picked up its pulse," Elena continued. "We found it among the crash site." She paused, allowing the gravity of her words to sink in.

"We were all so excited with our find that we didn't consider the existence of the creature based on its footprints in the snow. Instead, we now know that it either ejected or was thrown from the craft." The team exchanged uneasy glances, the implications of Elena's words dawning on them.

"Please go on, Elena," Dr. Silva said. "Are you suggesting that we should have spent more time searching for the creature who obviously survived the crash instead of focusing on the relic?"

Elena nodded. "Yes. We were so focused on the relic, we didn't stop to think that something might have survived the crash."

"And now it's here, trying to get it back," Captain Mitchell said, realizing the full extent of their situation.

"Elena is right. We underestimated it," Alice added somberly. "We assumed it was just some sort of artifact, not something that was being sought after."

"Or worse, something that was protecting it," Captain Mitchell said, his voice filled with concern.

"Which means it might not be acting alone," Dr. Silva said, his concern growing. "There could be more of them, or it could be trying to communicate with others."

"Exactly," Elena said firmly. "And if it's trying to communicate, it might be getting help or instructions on what to do next. In other words, what if each time it attacks, that information is being shared with other creatures?"

"We need to rethink our strategy," Alice said determinedly. "It's not just about capturing or killing the creature. We need to understand its motives and prepare for the possibility that it's not alone."

Captain Mitchell nodded. "Well, that changes everything. Instead of focusing on only one creature, we need to know if there are more." The team, now fully awake and alert, dispersed to their tasks with renewed urgency and determination, understanding the stakes had just been raised significantly. Dr. Lee rejoined the group, ready to contribute to their revised strategy.

Dr. Lee entered the room, his face etched with fatigue. "Sorry, I couldn't sleep. Any updates I missed?"

Captain Mitchell looked up from the map he was studying and glanced at his watch. "It's been over 24 hours since the last attack, giving us a chance to brainstorm. Elena pointed out that in all the excitement the day we found the relic, we didn't consider the possible existence of a surviving creature."

Dr. Lee frowned, trying to grasp the significance. "Sorry, I don't follow. So what? We now know of its existence."

Captain Mitchell leaned forward, his expression serious. "Elena brought up the possibility that perhaps there is more than one creature we are battling."

Dr. Lee's eyes widened with excitement. "You mean, we may have multiple alien beings we are dealing with?"

Captain Mitchell nodded. "Exactly. We need to think this through. Splitting up is risky, but it might be our only shot at finding its hiding place and understanding its behavior."

Dr. Silva agreed. "If we do decide to split up, we need a solid plan and constant communication. No one goes out of range."

Alice chimed in thoughtfully, "We can set up base points and have check-ins every fifteen minutes. If anyone finds anything, we regroup immediately."

Captain Mitchell, resolute, said, “Alright. Let’s prepare for a scouting mission. We’ll need enough supplies and equipment to stay safe and maintain communication.”

Dr. Lee, determined, added, “We should also prepare for any encounters. Tranquilizers, flamethrowers, flares—anything that can help us subdue or fend off the creature if we come across it.”

Captain Mitchell turned serious. “Agreed. But what would really work is some explosives.” He looked over to one of the security team members. “Any ideas?”

A security team member smiled. “We might be able to come up with something.”

Captain Mitchell addressed the team, his voice steady. “Alright. We leave at first light. I’ll decide who stays behind to guard the fort, while the rest of us go hunting.” The team nodded, understanding the gravity of the situation. They dispersed to gather their gear and finalize preparations for the scouting mission, tension and anticipation palpable.

The team gathered around a large table in the lab. Maps and equipment spread out before them. The atmosphere was tense but focused. Captain Mitchell stood at the head of the table, addressing the group.

“Alright, we’ve discussed our options and need to split up. Dr. Warren, Dr. Lee, and I, along with a few members of the security team, will search from the crash site to see if we can find a cave where the creature or creatures may be hiding.”

Alice nodded. "The rest of you will stay here at the research center, maintain communication, and be ready for anything. We'll need constant updates on the weather and any signs of activity." She looked at Elena, who nodded in agreement.

Dr. Silva added, his tone serious, "We'll hold the fort here. Make sure you check in every fifteen minutes. We can't afford to lose contact."

Dr. Lee, gearing up, emphasized, "We need to be prepared for anything out there. Everyone, make sure you have your equipment ready – tranquilizers, flares, and communication devices."

Captain Mitchell nodded. "Agreed. We head out at first light. Until then, get some rest and gather everything we might need. This mission is critical."

Alice looked around, her eyes serious. "Stay alert, everyone. The creature has been unpredictable so far, and we need to be ready for any surprises. Let's assume it can read our minds so we have to react accordingly with our thoughts."

A security team member, confident, added, "We're ready, Captain."

Captain Mitchell, grim, replied, "Good. Let's move out. We need to hurry. Daybreak is almost here. The team members gathered their gear, checking equipment and packing supplies. The sense of urgency and anticipation was evident in their focus.

The first light of dawn broke over the horizon. Captain Mitchell, Alice, Dr. Lee, and the security team assembled outside, ready to embark on their mission. "Remember," Captain Mitchell said seriously, "stay sharp and stick together. We move as one unit and maintain communication at all times."

Alice nodded, her expression determined. "Let's find that cave and put an end to this."

Dr. Lee, ready and resolute, added, "We'll be careful and thorough. Let's go." The team set off, leaving the research facility behind. Those staying behind watched them go, the weight of the mission heavy on everyone's shoulders.

CHAPTER 13

The search team trudged through the harsh, frozen landscape, following Captain Mitchell. Visibility was low, the icy wind whipping around them. The sound of their footsteps crunching in the snow was the only noise piercing the eerie silence. Captain Mitchell shouted over the wind, "Stay close! We don't want to get separated!"

The team members, including Alice, Dr. Lee, and the security personnel, nodded and tightened their formation. The cold was biting, and their breath formed clouds in the frigid air. They finally reached the crash site, marked by twisted metal and scattered debris. The area was desolate, remnants of the alien craft buried in snow.

Alice pointed toward a spot in the snow. "We found footprints over there on the day we discovered the relic." The team spread out cautiously, ensuring they could still see the shoulders of the person next to them. They advanced slowly, scanning the ground and the surroundings.

"I can barely make anything out in this weather," a security team member said, struggling to see.

Captain Mitchell, determined, responded, "Keep looking. We're close, I can feel it." They continued to search, moving methodically through the snow. Just as they were about to give up, Captain Mitchell spotted something in the distance.

"There!" Captain Mitchell exclaimed, pointing excitedly. "I think that's a cave."

The team quickly gathered around him, peering through the blowing snow. Indeed, a dark opening in the rocky landscape was visible ahead. Dr. Marcus Lee, relieved, said, "We found it."

Captain Mitchell's expression turned serious. "Alright, here's the plan. We'll approach carefully and set the makeshift bomb near the entrance. We need to be quick and quiet. Dr. Warren, you and Dr. Lee cover us while we set it up."

Alice nodded. "Understood. We'll keep an eye out for any movement."

A security team member readied their equipment. "Let's do this." The team advanced toward the cave, moving slowly and deliberately. The tension was high, each step taking them closer to a potential encounter with the creature. They reached the entrance of the cave, the darkness inside seeming to swallow the light.

Captain Mitchell whispered, "Sounds like there is more than one creature in there. Set the bomb here, just inside the entrance. Make sure it's secure. Set the timer for five minutes to give us enough time to retreat."

The security team member knelt down and carefully began to set the makeshift bomb, his hands steady despite the cold and nerves. Dr. Lee leaned in and whispered to Alice, "This is it. We need to be ready for anything."

Alice whispered back, "Stay sharp. We've come too far to lose now."

Captain Mitchell quietly instructed, "Everyone, take your positions. Once the bomb is set, we move back and detonate."

The team members took their positions, weapons at the ready, eyes fixed on the cave entrance. The bomb was finally set, and the security team member gave a thumbs-up. "Good," Mitchell whispered. "Now let's move back, nice and easy."

The team retreated a safe distance, keeping their eyes on the cave. The tension was palpable, every second feeling like an eternity as they prepared for whatever came next. The team crouched at a safe distance, anxiously watching the cave entrance. The cold wind continued to blow, but the tension kept them focused.

"Everyone, stay sharp," Captain Mitchell whispered. "It should go off any moment now." The seconds ticked by slowly. Everyone's breath was visible in the cold air, and the silence was almost unbearable.

"How much longer?" Dr. Alice Warren asked nervously.

"Any second now," a security team member replied quietly. Suddenly, a movement caught their eye. A creature emerged from the darkness of the cave, its form barely visible through the swirling snow.

"Look, it's coming out!" Dr. Lee whispered urgently. The creature stood near the bomb, initially unaware of its presence. The team held their breath, watching intently.

"Hold steady. Wait for it..." Captain Mitchell whispered. The creature moved closer to the bomb, its alien features partially visible. It seemed curious, sniffing the air, and then it noticed the device. It reached down to examine it.

"Come on, come on..." Alice whispered. The creature's fingers touched the bomb, and in that instant, the device detonated. A blinding flash of light and a deafening explosion tore through the air, throwing the creature backward.

The explosion was massive, ripping the creature to pieces and sending chunks of rock and debris flying. The shockwave knocked the team back slightly, but they quickly recovered. "Take cover!" Captain Mitchell shouted over the noise.

The team shielded themselves as debris rained down. When the dust settled, they looked up to see the cave entrance collapsed, rocks and rubble blocking the way. “Did we get it?” Alice asked, stunned.

Dr. Lee observed the debris. “It looks like it. The entrance is sealed.”

“What about the creature?” a security team member asked, looking around.

Captain Mitchell replied grimly, “It’s in pieces. We got it.” The team slowly stood, the realization of their success sinking in. They moved closer to the cave entrance, carefully avoiding the still-smoking debris.

“Stop! Don’t go any closer. Let’s get back to the research facility and regroup,” Captain Mitchell said determinedly. “We need to reassess and plan our next move.” The team nodded and began to make their way back, their spirits slightly lifted by their small victory.

The room was filled with music and laughter as everyone congratulated each other. Captain Mitchell left the group briefly but soon returned carrying several bottles of champagne. “I think we’ve all earned a little bubbly,” he announced with a grin.

Cheers rang out as some security team members popped open the champagne and started pouring. Dr. Silva approached Alice with a smile. “Dr. Warren, may I have this dance?”

Alice smiled back. “Well, Dr. Silva, I thought you’d never ask.” The two began dancing, and more cheers filled the room.

Sunlight streamed into the cave from an opening on the opposite side of the explosion site. The interior was dimly lit, with shadows dancing across the walls. Snow and debris covered the floor, remnants of the explosion still settling.

A mound of snow near the center of the cave began to shift. Slowly, a creature's hand pushed through the snow, followed by its entire form as it struggled to free itself. The creature rose, shaking off the snow and debris, revealing its menacing features.

CHAPTER 14

The creature surveyed the cave, its eyes falling upon the bodies of other creatures, including several smaller ones that appeared to be babies, lifeless and partially buried under the snow and rubble. The sight enraged the creature, a deep, guttural growl emanating from its chest.

Its gaze shifted to the source of the sunlight, a narrow hole in the cave wall where the explosion had created an opening. The creature moved toward the hole, its powerful claws scraping against the rocky surface. It started clawing at the edges of the hole, trying to widen it, driven by a desperate need to escape and seek revenge.

Chunks of rock and ice broke away as the creature continued to claw at the opening, its roars growing louder and more intense. The sunlight glinted off its dark, alien skin, highlighting the raw power and anger coursing through it.

Pausing for a moment, the creature looked back at the fallen bodies of its kin. Its eyes narrowed with a newfound resolve, a fierce determination to avenge their deaths. It turned back to the opening, renewing its efforts with even greater ferocity.

As the creature clawed at the hole, more sunlight poured into the cave, illuminating the tragic scene. The creature's roars echoed through the mountains, a chilling reminder of the danger that still lurked.

With one final, mighty effort, the creature widened the hole enough to squeeze through. It emerged into the blinding daylight, its menacing form casting a long shadow over the snow. The creature paused, taking in its new surroundings, then let out a deafening roar that reverberated through the landscape. It was a roar of grief, fury, and a vow for retribution.

Assembled in the dining room, several hours had passed and a sense of relief and camaraderie filled the air. The room was filled with the comforting aroma of a home-cooked meal. Captain Tom Mitchell walked in, smiling. "Well, chef, what culinary treats do you have for us tonight?"

The chef grinned. "Well, Captain, in celebration of our victory, I've made my famous spaghetti and meatballs, plus garlic bread, salad, and, pardon my pun, a monster chocolate cake." The team laughed, the tension from earlier easing into light-hearted banter. They began to serve themselves, filling their plates with the delicious food. Alice and Captain Mitchell sat next to each other, their shoulders brushing as they ate.

"This is exactly what we needed," Alice said, smiling. "A little comfort food goes a long way."

Captain Mitchell nodded. "Couldn't agree more. It's nice to have a moment of normalcy." The team chatted and joked, enjoying the rare moment of peace. As the meal wound down, the mood turned more reflective.

"It's hard to believe we actually did it," Dr. Lee said with a sigh. "But we can't let our guard down. There could be more out there."

Captain Mitchell responded seriously, "You're right. We'll stay vigilant. But tonight, let's just appreciate what we've accomplished." As the team finished their meal, they started to disperse, heading to their quarters to rest. Alice and Captain Mitchell lingered a bit longer, sharing a quiet moment. Alice leaned in, her voice a whisper. "Tom, can we talk for a minute? In private?"

Captain Mitchell nodded. "Of course." They entered a small, cozy room adjacent to the hallway. The room was dimly lit, the soft glow creating an intimate atmosphere. Alice closed the door behind them. She turned to face Tom, her eyes searching his.

"I don't know what I'd do if something happened to you out there," she said softly. "It made me realize how much you mean to me."

Captain Mitchell took her hand, his gaze steady. "I feel the same way, Alice. This whole experience... it's brought a lot of things into focus for me." They moved closer, the space between them shrinking. Their eyes locked, and in a moment of shared understanding, they embraced.

"Tom..." Alice breathed.

"Alice..." Tom whispered. They kissed, the intensity of their emotions pouring into the moment. Slowly, they made their way to the bed, the world outside fading away.

The room they shared was dimly lit by the moonlight streaming through a boarded-up window. Alice and Captain Mitchell lay in bed together, wrapped in each other's arms, a sense of peace and connection enveloping them. "Do you think we got them all?" Alice asked softly.

Tom kissed her forehead and stroked her hair. "Whatever was in that cave was blown to hell," he said gently. "Even if the blast didn't kill them, tons of snow and debris sealed whatever else was in there until another research team decides to excavate the cave."

Alice sighed, a mixture of relief and lingering concern. "I hope you're right. I just can't shake the feeling that we might have missed something."

Tom spoke soothingly, "We did everything we could, Alice. We'll stay vigilant and be ready for anything. But for now, try to rest. We need our strength for whatever comes next."

Alice smiled slightly. "You're right. I'll try." They lay together in silence for a moment, the weight of their experiences settling over them.

The following morning and late into the afternoon nothing eventful occurred. Captain Mitchell felt it was best to give the team a day off to process what they had gone through. As night approached and everyone started to consider bed, in the dimly lit hallway, Dr. Lee sneaks out of his quarters, carrying a small, secure case. He glances around, ensuring no one sees him, and quietly makes his way toward the lab. He enters the lab and locks the door behind him.

He places the case on a table and opens it, revealing the vial of the creature's blood he had hidden earlier. He stares at it, a mixture of fascination and determination in his eyes. "This is just the beginning," he whispers to himself. "There's so much we can learn from this." He carefully secures the vial back in the case, planning his next steps. His thoughts are interrupted by a faint noise from outside.

Back in the private room, Alice stirs, sensing something amiss. "Did you hear that?" Alice asks, frowning.

Captain Mitchell listens intently. "Yeah, I did. Stay here, I'll check it out."

"No, I'm coming with you. We stick together, remember? They quickly got dressed and headed out of the room, moving cautiously through the facility. They walked down the hallway, alert to any unusual sounds or movements. As they approached the lab, they saw a faint light under the door.

Captain Mitchell whispers to Alice. "Someone's in there. Stay behind me. He found the door locked. Inside, Dr. Lee panicked with the case on the table. He tried to remain calm before opening the door.

"What are you doing, Marcus?

Dr. Lee is startled. "Tom, Alice... I can explain."

"You'd better. What's going on?" Captain Mitchell asks.

Dr. Lee, defensive, looks at both Alice and Tom. "I was just... making sure we had everything secured. This blood could be crucial for our research."

"And you couldn't do that during the day, with everyone else around?" Captain Mitchell asks.

"Fine. I was curious. I wanted to run some tests, see if there's anything we missed. This could be a breakthrough, Tom. We can't let fear stop us from learning."

Alice spoke cautiously, "We understand, Marcus. But you need to remember, safety comes first. If there's more to discover, we'll do it together, following protocols."

Captain Mitchell added decisively, "Exactly. Now, secure that vial and get some rest. We'll discuss this in the morning."

Dr. Lee nodded reluctantly, placing the vial back into the case and locking it securely. "Alright. I'm sorry. I'll see you both in the morning," he said quietly.

Captain Mitchell and Alice watched as Dr. Lee left the lab, then exchanged a concerned look before heading back to their quarters. As Dr. Lee left the lab and headed to his quarters, Alice and Captain Mitchell shared a concerned look. "We need to keep an eye on him,"

Alice sighed. "Curiosity is one thing, but this..."

Captain Mitchell nodded. "Agreed. We can't afford any more risks. Let's get some rest and be ready for whatever comes next." They headed back to their individual quarters, the sense of unease lingering but tempered by their resolve to face whatever lay ahead together.

Suddenly, alarms blared and red lights filled the research facility, rousing anyone who was asleep. Captain Mitchell sprang into action, running to the command post.

CHAPTER 15

Captain Mitchell brought the team together in the command center. "Report."

Elena pointed to several video monitors. "Captain, the creature has broken into the containment building. Look." On the screens, the creature was visible, seemingly searching for something. Dr. Silva, Alice, and Dr. Lee entered, their eyes fixed on the displays.

"It's looking for the relic," Alice said.

"It looks pissed to me," Captain Mitchell replied. On cue, the creature began throwing objects from tables, smashing lab equipment, and snarling. It then exited through the hole it had made in the wall.

Dr. Lee observed, "Well, we know that at least one of them survived the explosion."

"What is the relic so damn important to it?" Elena wondered aloud.

Alice responded, "We may never know, but now that it knows the relic is not working anymore, I'm sure we are its new targets." Unnoticed by the others, Dr. Lee abruptly left the room.

"Elena, can you bring up the footage from the blast yesterday?" Captain Mitchell asked.

"Sure. Give me a few moments," Elena replied. Soon, one of the monitors lit up with footage showing the cave before, during, and after the explosion.

"Look, there," Captain Mitchell pointed. Everyone strained to see the area he was indicating on the monitor.

"I see it," Elena said. "There's an opening near the top of the mound. One of the creatures survived the blast and use the hole to dig itself out."

Dr. Lee's bedroom had been converted into a makeshift lab. A table was cluttered with a microscope and various lab equipment. Dr. Lee carefully took out a small sample of the creature's blood and placed it under the microscope, seemingly unconcerned about the creature breaking into the containment building.

"Perhaps once I'm out of this place, I can allow these cells to replicate," he muttered to himself. "Who knows? Under the right conditions, I might be able to create a fully grown creature." He examined the blood sample intently, lost in his thoughts of scientific discovery and ambition.

The team turned back to the exit spot the creature had used to leave the containment building.

"Elena, turn on all cameras outside. Let's see where our friend is," Captain Mitchell instructed. Elena masterfully switched from one camera to another until they spotted movement in the center of the complex.

"That's the food and supplies area. We can't let it get in there," Mitchell said.

As soon as he spoke, the creature crashed through the wall and began trashing the room, throwing much-needed supplies and materials around. Captain Mitchell looked at his security team members.

"Never mind. It's too late. We need to implement the trap to electrocute this asshole. Dr. Silva, do you have the virus ready?"

Dr. Silva nodded. "If you can render it unconscious for only a few seconds, I think I can spray more than enough virus onto it."

Alice interjected, "Tom, I think we can manipulate the creature to the exact area we need it in. Elena and I recreated the pulsing sound that came from the relic. If we set the trap, I can replay the sounds to attract it to the area."

Captain Mitchell nodded. "Alright everyone, listen up. Dr. Silva, besides me, Elena, and Dr. Warren, who else appears to have the flu?" Dr. Silva looked around the room, pointing to several of the security team members.

"Good. Here's what we are going to do. You three will be in a room adjacent to the trap. Before entering, Dr. Warren will turn on the sounds. It will avoid the room we are in and should focus on the trap. Once it steps on the conductors, I will throw the switch, hopefully frying the bastard. Once it's stunned, Dr. Silva will enter and spray the creature, then return back inside the room with us."

From outside, the growling of the creature was heard as it destroyed their supplies. Elena looked at the video screen, watching the creature's movements intently.

"He just went back outside and is headed off into the snowbank," Elena reported.

"It will be back," Alice said.

"Alright, let's move. We don't have much time," Captain Mitchell urged urgently.

Alice, Dr. Silva, and the rest of the team hurriedly moved into the adjacent room, their faces tense with anxiety as they set up the trap. Each member worked with a practiced efficiency, the gravity of their situation evident in their swift, coordinated actions.

Alice whispered to herself, her breath coming in short, nervous bursts. "Come on, come on..." She flipped a switch, and a series of high-pitched frequencies filled the air, designed specifically to lure the creature. The sound waves seemed to vibrate through the walls, drawing ever closer the ominous growls that echoed through the facility.

"We need to move," Alice urged, leading the team into a secured room where those afflicted with the flu were already gathered. She could feel the tension in the air, every muscle in her body tight with anticipation.

Captain Tom Mitchell's voice crackled through the radio, calm but firm. "Positions, everyone. Get ready."

From the safety of the adjacent room, the team watched the trap room with bated breath. The creature's powerful form crashed through an exterior wall, debris scattering across the floor. It paused, ears twitching, sniffing the air suspiciously. The lure had worked; it was in the trap room.

"Wait for it..." Captain Mitchell whispered, his eyes never leaving the creature. Just as the creature stepped onto the conductors, a figure suddenly burst through a side entrance. Dr. Marcus Lee, his face a mix of desperation and determination, ran towards the creature.

"Wait! Don't hurt it! We can learn from it!" he shouted, his voice filled with an almost frantic urgency.

Captain Mitchell's voice rose in panic. "Lee, get back here!" Ignoring the captain's desperate plea, Dr. Lee continued his approach, his hands outstretched in a gesture of peace.

"Please," he implored the creature, "we don't have to fight. We can coexist. We can understand each other." The room fell silent, the tension so thick it was almost tangible. Every eye was on Dr. Lee and the creature, waiting to see what would happen next.

The creature tilted its head, its movements momentarily paused by Dr. Lee's words. For a brief second, hope flickered in the air. Then, with terrifying speed, it lashed out. Its massive claws sliced through the air, decapitating Dr. Lee in one swift, brutal motion. His body crumpled to the floor, lifeless.

"Now!" Captain Mitchell bellowed, his voice a mix of rage and desperation. He slammed the switch down. A powerful surge of electricity shot through the creature, making it roar in pain and confusion. Its body convulsed, movements becoming erratic and uncoordinated. It thrashed wildly before collapsing first to its knees and then onto its stomach, immobilized but still breathing.

"Now, Dr. Silva, go!" Captain Mitchell commanded, urgency in his tone. Dr. Frank Silva, gripping a sprayer filled with the virus, stepped into the room cautiously. His heart pounded, but his hands remained steady. He approached the creature, its labored breaths echoing in the silence.

"This is for all the people you've killed..." he murmured, voice barely audible.

He sprayed the creature methodically, ensuring the virus coated every part of its body. The creature writhed under the spray, its attempts to move ineffective against the paralyzing shock.

"Silva, get back here!" Captain Mitchell's voice cut through the tension, urgent and commanding. Dr. Silva retreated swiftly, rejoining the team in the adjacent room. They slammed the door shut behind him, sealing themselves in. The air was thick with a mix of relief and lingering fear, their eyes on the door, waiting to see if their desperate plan had worked.

Alice, breathless and wide-eyed, looked around at her team. “Did it work?” she asked, her voice tinged with hope and fear.

Captain Mitchell, his face set in serious lines, replied, “We’ll find out soon enough. Everyone, stay alert.”

They all turned their attention to the monitors. The creature, still convulsing from the shock, began to weaken as the virus took hold. Thick mucus oozed from its mouth, eyes, and ears. Finally, its massive form collapsed, motionless.

Dr. Silva exhaled deeply, his relief palpable. “We did it… we actually did it.”

Captain Mitchell placed a reassuring hand on Silva’s shoulder. “Good work, everyone. But we’re not out of the woods yet. Let’s keep an eye on it and make sure it’s really down for good.”

The team nodded, their relief tempered by caution. They continued to watch the monitors intently, ready for any signs of movement. The creature lay still on the cold floor, the virus having done its job. The team approached cautiously, weapons at the ready, ensuring it was truly dead.

Captain Mitchell gave the final order. “Alright, let’s make sure this thing is really done for. Security team, cut off its head and take the body to the largest walk-in freezer. We’re not taking any chances.”

The security team, armed with heavy-duty equipment, nodded in agreement. They moved in and carefully severed the creature's head. With meticulous precision, they lifted both the head and the body onto stretchers, ensuring they were secure before transporting them to the freezer. The team's movements were deliberate, their focus unwavering, knowing that their safety depended on these final actions.

CHAPTER 16

The security team wheeled the creature's remains down the dimly lit hallway, the eerie silence broken only by the clatter of their equipment. Each step echoed ominously, a reminder of the night's harrowing events. Arriving at the walk-in freezer, the team carefully placed the creature's head and body inside. They ensured the door was tightly locked, securing the gruesome contents within the freezing cold.

Captain Mitchell and Alice stood together in the command center, the weight of recent events heavy on their shoulders. Captain Mitchell's expression was a mix of frustration and sadness as he looked at Alice.

"If Dr. Lee had just gone along with the plan, he would have had his dream... an almost intact creature. His obsession cost him his life," Captain Mitchell said, his voice laced with regret.

Alice sighed, her gaze distant. "He couldn't see past his ambition. It's a harsh reminder of what's at stake out here."

Captain Mitchell placed a reassuring hand on her shoulder. "We did what we had to do. Now, let's focus on getting everyone out of here safely." The remaining research team members gathered in the command center, the atmosphere tense but hopeful. Elena worked at the console, her fingers flying over the keys with practiced speed.

"We've got our comms back up! Our rescue team will arrive in five hours," Elena announced excitedly. A wave of relief washed over the team. They exchanged smiles and sighs of relief, the end of their ordeal finally in sight.

"Thank goodness. We'll finally be out of this nightmare," Dr. Silva said, sneezing.

Alice smiled. "Guess who has the flu now?" Everyone laughed, the tension in the room dissipating for a moment.

"It's almost over. Just a few more hours," Alice added, her smile brightening the room.

Captain Mitchell stood with Alice. "You all did an incredible job. Let's start preparing for their arrival." The team dispersed to make preparations, but Captain Mitchell and Alice lingered for a moment longer. Captain Mitchell pulled Alice into an embrace.

"We made it, Alice," he said softly. As he looked around, he noticed most of the staff smiling at them. "Oops. I guess our secret is out of the bag."

Alice laughed. "I think everyone knew long before we did. It was the worst kept secret." They both laughed, sharing a quiet, tender moment. Finding solace in each other, they looked forward to their rescue, the promise of safety and a new beginning just hours away.

FAMOUS SCENES

PRODUCTION

In 1950, Charles Lederer and Ben Hecht persuaded Howard Hawks to purchase the rights to John W. Campbell's novella "Who Goes There?" for $1,250.

In an unusual practice for the era, no actors were named during the film's dramatic opening title sequence, which featured "slow burning letters through background"; the cast credits appeared at the end of the film. George Fenneman, who had a small role, was gaining fame as Groucho Marx's announcer on the popular quiz show "You Bet Your Life" at the time. Fenneman later mentioned he had difficulty with the film's overlapping dialogue.

The film was partly shot in Glacier National Park, with interior sets built at a Los Angeles ice storage plant. The scene where the alien is set on fire and repeatedly doused with kerosene was one of the first full-body fire stunts ever filmed.

The film leveraged the national sentiment in America at the time to enhance its horror elements. It reflected post-Hiroshima skepticism about science and the prevailing negative views of scientists who meddled with things better left alone. In the end, it is American servicemen and several sensible scientists who triumph over the alien invader.

SCREENPLAY

The screenplay, loosely adapted by Charles Lederer with uncredited rewrites from Howard Hawks and Ben Hecht, was based on the 1938 novella "Who Goes There?" by John W. Campbell. The story was first published in "Astounding Science Fiction" under Campbell's pseudonym, Don A. Stuart. Science fiction author A. E. van Vogt, who had been inspired by reading "Who Goes There?" and was a prolific contributor to "Astounding," had wanted to write the script.

The screenplay changes the fundamental nature of the alien from Campbell's novella. Instead of a life form capable of assuming the physical and mental characteristics of any living thing it encounters (as realized in John Carpenter's 1982 adaptation, "The Thing"), the alien is portrayed as a humanoid life form with a cellular structure closer to vegetation, requiring blood to survive. This plant-like structure makes it impervious to bullets but not to other destructive forces such as fire and electricity.

DIRECTION

There is debate over whether the film was directed by Howard Hawks, with Christian Nyby receiving the credit to obtain his Director's Guild membership, or whether Nyby directed it with considerable input from producer Hawks for Hawks' Winchester Pictures, which released the film through RKO Radio Pictures Inc. Hawks gave Nyby only $5,460 of RKO's $50,000 director's fee and kept the rest, but Hawks always denied directing the film.

Cast members had differing opinions on Hawks' and Nyby's contributions. Kenneth Tobey claimed that "Hawks directed it, all except one scene," while George Fenneman stated that "Hawks would once in a while direct, if he had an idea, but it was Chris' show." Robert Cornthwaite noted that "Chris always deferred to Hawks... Maybe because he did defer to him, people misinterpreted it."

William Self, one of the film's stars who later became President of 20th Century Fox Television, described the production, saying, "Chris was the director in our eyes, but Howard was the boss in our eyes." Although Self acknowledged that "Hawks was directing the picture from the sidelines," he also noted that "Chris would stage each scene, how to play it. But then he would go over to Howard and ask him for advice, which the actors did not hear... Even though I was there every day, I don't think any of us can answer the question. Only Chris and Howard can answer the question."

At a reunion of "The Thing" cast and crew members in 1982, Nyby addressed the question directly: "Did Hawks direct it? That's one of the most inane and ridiculous questions I've ever heard, and people keep asking. That it was Hawks' style. Of course it was. This is a man I studied and wanted to be like. You would certainly emulate and copy the master you're sitting under, which I did. Anyway, if you're taking painting lessons from Rembrandt, you don't take the brush out of the master's hands."

"The Thing from Another World" was released in April 1951. By the end of the year, it had accrued $1,950,000 in distributors' domestic rentals (U.S. and Canada), making it the 46th biggest earner of the year. It outperformed all other science fiction films released that year, including "The Day the Earth Stood Still" and "When Worlds Collide."

CRITICAL RECEPTION

Bosley Crowther of The New York Times remarked, "Taking a fantastic notion (or is it, really?), Mr. Hawks has developed a movie that is generous with thrills and chills... Adults and children can have a lot of old-fashioned movie fun at 'The Thing', but parents should understand their children and think twice before letting them see this film if their emotions are not properly conditioned."

In contrast, "Gene" of Variety criticized the film for lacking "genuine entertainment values." In 1973, science fiction editor and publisher Lester del Rey compared the film unfavorably to its source material, calling it "just another monster epic, totally lacking in the force and tension of the original story." Isaac Asimov went so far as to consider it one of the worst movies he had ever seen. John W. Campbell, the author of the original story, acknowledged that an adaptation would need to alter elements from the source material, which he considered too frightening for most audiences. He hoped, however, that the film would at least spark an interest in science fiction.

LEGACY AND MODERN RECEPTION

Over time, "The Thing from Another World" has come to be regarded as one of the best films of 1951 and a seminal science fiction film of the 1950s. It holds an 87% "Fresh" rating on Rotten Tomatoes from 68 reviews, with the consensus noting that the film "is better than most flying saucer movies, thanks to well-drawn characters and concise, tense plotting."

In 2001, the United States Library of Congress deemed the film "culturally significant" and selected it for preservation in the National Film Registry. Time magazine has also lauded "The Thing from Another World," naming it "the greatest 1950s sci-fi movie."

FILM POSTERS

Pacific DRIVE-IN THEATRES
Tri-City DRIVE-IN Theatre
BETWEEN COLTON and REDLANDS
HWY 99
Phone S. B. 8-2971
or Redlands 2-6722
BOX OFFICE OPENS 7:00 P. M. — SHOW BEGINS AT DUSK
FIRST With the BEST for the LEAST
TERRIFYING!
"IT'S ALIVE, I TELL YOU... I SHOT IT SIX TIMES, BUT IT CAME AFTER ME!"
THE THING
FROM ANOTHER WORLD!
Also
JACK CARSON · JANIS PAIGE
"MR. UNIVERSE"
KIDDIES'
WONDER PLAYGROUND

James Arness as the Thing

OTHER HORROR NOVELS BY THE AUTHOR:

"HOUSE ON HAUNTED HILL RESURRECTION"

"House on Haunted Hill: Resurrection" is a contemporary reimagining of the iconic Vincent Price horror film. After serving a twenty-year sentence for his wife's murder in the notorious House on Haunted Hill, Frederick Loren decides to host another haunted house party with a sinister agenda—to expose several self-proclaimed psychics as frauds. Seven individuals, each harboring their own flaws, eagerly accept Loren's invitation, enticed by the promise of a $100,000 prize if they survive the night.

Unbeknownst to the guests, the mansion's previous owner, Watson Pritchard, firmly believes in its haunted nature, and his convictions prove chillingly accurate. The malevolent spirit of Inquisitor Torquemada, along with his bloodthirsty henchmen, awakens from its slumber after years of dormancy, fixating its supernatural wrath on the unsuspecting guests.

"THE TINGLER UNLEASHED"

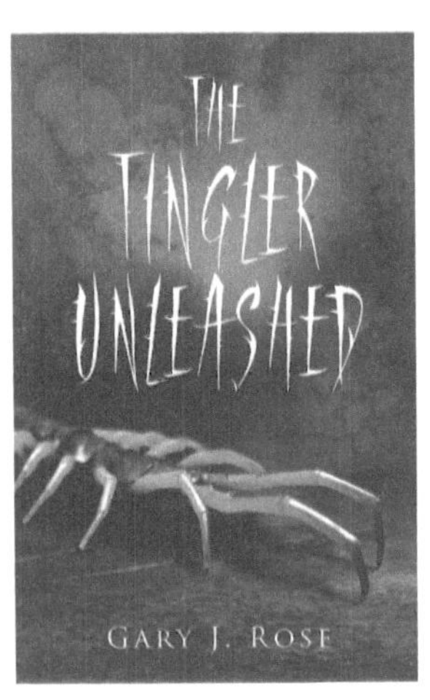

Within the pages of this cover lies "The Tingler Unleashed," a contemporary reimagining that pays homage to the 1959 cinematic masterpiece by William Castle, featuring the incomparable Vincent Price. The film's narrative revolves around a brilliant scientist unraveling the existence of a peculiar parasite dwelling within humans, christened the "tingler." This minuscule entity thrives on fear, inducing a spine-tingling sensation in its host whenever terror strikes.

Dr. Warren Chapin, a dedicated pathologist, unearths the truth behind the spine-tingling phenomenon, attributing it to the growth of a peculiar creature residing within every human—an aptly named "tingler." This parasitic entity attaches itself to the spinal cord, coiling, feeding, and gaining strength in response to fear, capable of rendering its host immobile by constricting the spine. Only the piercing release of a scream can thwart its deadly embrace.

Transporting us to the year 2023, in the enigmatic town of Raven's Hollow, this novel propels us into a future still haunted by the echoes of events that transpired over half a century ago.

"BENEATH THE EARTH"

"Beneath the Earth" is a gripping horror/science fiction novel that combines the thrill of exploration with the terror of supernatural creatures. Set in the desolate landscape of Russia, a group of American scientists find themselves plunged into a nightmarish battle for survival when they venture into the depths of the abandoned Kola Superdeep Borehole.

When seismic activity causes the long-forgotten borehole to erupt, it releases a malevolent force into the world - gigantic acid-spewing spiders that have lurked beneath the Earth's surface for centuries. As the creatures emerge from the depths, the Russian government urgently requests the expertise of American scientists to assess the situation and contain the growing threat.

Driven by a mix of scientific curiosity and a desire to prevent a potential global catastrophe, the team descends into the uncharted darkness. Battling their way through hordes of terrifying spiders, the scientists enter the lair of these nightmarish creatures, only to stumble upon a shocking discovery.

"CARNIVAL OF LOST SOULS"

"Step into the eerie world of 'Carnival of Lost Souls,' a contemporary reimagining of the 1962 American psychological horror film 'Carnival of Souls.' In a chilling twist of fate, our female protagonist survives a harrowing car accident, only to find herself teetering on the precipice of sanity. Haunting hallucinations beckon her to a long-forgotten, desolate carnival ground, where an insidious serial killer lurks in the shadows, determined to snuff out her life.

Sixty-one years later the tale is reborn with a fresh layer of suspense and intrigue. The carnival remains abandoned, or does it? What sinister secrets lie beneath the rusted rides and faded banners, and where have all the missing souls vanished to? Brace yourself for a riveting journey into the unknown as the shocking truth unravels, unearthing the chilling mysteries that have haunted this forsaken carnival for decades."

"13 GHOSTS AWAKENED"

In "13 Ghosts Awakened," the chilling legacy of Dr. Plato Zorba looms large over a contemporary setting, setting the stage for a harrowing journey into the unknown.

Dr. Sullivan, a renowned skeptic psychologist with a knack for debunking fraudulent spiritualists, finds himself thrust into a world of the supernatural when he's approached by the last surviving member of the Zorba family. Tasked with ridding the infamous Zorba mansion of its spectral inhabitants, Dr. Sullivan reluctantly agrees, drawn by the challenge and his thirst for unraveling the mysteries of the mind.

Accompanied by a team of five intrepid students, each with their own reasons for delving into the unknown, Dr. West enters the dilapidated mansion under the guise of a scientific study. But as they step across the threshold, they unwittingly trigger a chain of events that awaken the dormant horrors within.

As the mansion comes alive with malevolent energy, the team discovers Dr. Zorba's journal, revealing the twisted experiments and obsessions that bound the spirits to the estate. Trapped within the labyrinthine corridors, they must navigate a deadly game of cat and mouse with the vengeful ghosts, each more terrifying than the last.

But the true horror lies in the revelation that Dr. Zorba's grip extends beyond the grave, his spectral presence determined to add the intruders to his collection. With time running out and their sanity hanging by a thread, Dr. Sullivan and his team must confront their own inner demons and unlock the secrets of the mansion before they become permanent residents in its haunted halls.

"THE BIRDS RETURN"

In the coastal city of Myrtle Beach, South Carolina, tranquility is shattered when flocks of birds launch menacing attacks on unsuspecting residents. These once-harmless creatures now carry an unsettling purpose, casting a shadow of fear over the community.

Dr. Lena Lawrence, an ornithologist grappling with the recent death of her retired police officer husband, seeks solace by sunbathing at Myrtle Beach State Park. Her peace is violently disrupted when she is attacked by a swarm of aggressive gulls. During the chaos, she is aided by Dr. Alex Sousa, a marine biologist who also falls victim to the avian assault.

The birds disappear as mysteriously as they had arrived, only to return repeatedly, launching simulated attacks that leave the town's residents in a state of constant terror. As the attacks escalate, Lena and Alex join forces to uncover the reason behind the birds' strange behavior. Their investigation reveals a web of hidden agendas, environmental crises, and personal struggles.

Inspired by the classic Alfred Hitchcock film "The Birds," this reimagined tale is a gripping narrative of survival, resilience, and the untamed power of nature. Will Lena and Alex find a way to stop the relentless avian onslaught, or will Myrtle Beach fall to the fury of the skies?

www.ingramcontent.com/pod-product-compliance
Lightning Source LLC
Chambersburg PA
CBHW020548310726
48979CB00008B/1133/J

* 9 7 9 8 9 9 0 7 2 5 4 2 3 *